THE PATH OF SHADOWS

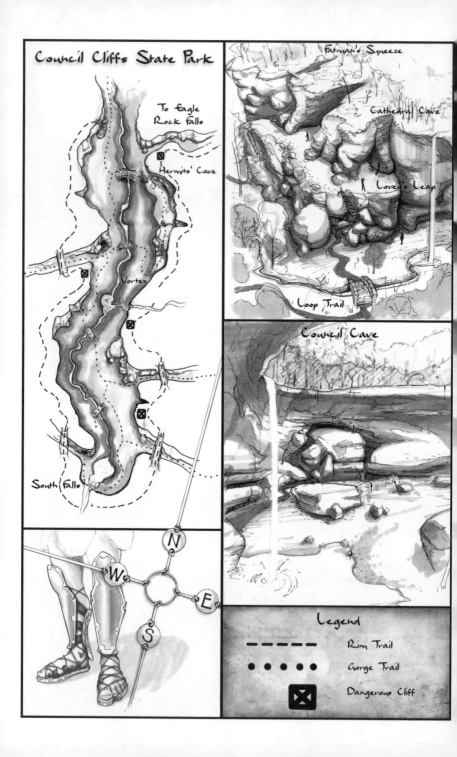

Elijah Creek & The Armor of God #4

THE PATH OF SHADOWS

Lena Wood

✳✳✳✳✳✳✳✳✳✳✳

Standard
PUBLISHING
Bringing The Word to Life

Project editor: Lindsay Black
Content editor: Amy Beveridge
Copy editor: Lynn Lusby Pratt
Cover and interior design: Robert Glover
Cover oil paintings: Lena Wood
Map illustration: Daniel Armstrong

Library of Congress Cataloging-in-Publication Data

Wood, Lena, 1950-
    The path of shadows / Lena Wood.
        p. cm. — (Elijah Creek & the Armor of God ; bk. 4)
    Summary: With only the flight of the raven to guide them, members of the
Elijah clan search for the shoes of peace, but as the group endures deception,
illness, and loss, Elijah undergoes a powerful prayer experience and his
relationship with God deepens.
    ISBN 0-7847-1759-1 (pbk.)
    [1. Christian life--Fiction. 2. Friendship--Fiction.] I. Title.
PZ7.W84973Pat 2005
[Fic]--dc22

                                                        2005010006

                        ISBN 0-7847-1759-1

    01 00 09 08 07 06 05   9 8 7 6 5 4 3 2 1

for **Arian** *and* **Andrea**,
we've walked the path

Deepest appreciation to:
Joy, *for courage to share her medical trials*
The Armstrongs, *for housing near "Council Cliffs"*
Cason Pratt, *for the nature center tour*
&
The Prince of Peace

Though I walk through the valley of the shadow of death,
I will fear no evil, for you are with me.

—Psalm 23:4

Chapter 1

SKID and Rob stretched out on the gazebo benches; I sat on the rail, propped my foot against the post, and looked out over Silver Lake. School was out—we were feeling free as birds, as lazy as old dogs. We now had the first three pieces of the armor of God in our possession: belt, breastplate, and shield. Three down, three to go. Summer spread out before us as wide and smooth as the lake.

Casually I said, "Our last sign was the raven cruising toward Council Cliffs. Not much to go on . . . Dowland could've dug a hole anywhere along a path and buried the next piece."

"Those trails go for miles," said Rob thoughtfully, his arms folded, his eyes drifting drowsily around the gazebo rafters.

Skid shrugged. "We have all summer."

"I'm not worried," I said.

Looking for the armor of God was a big part of our lives now, even though we'd only started last fall. Reece had predicted that the quest would change my life, and she was right. Sure, I still had lots of regular duties at Camp Mudjokivi: pool cleaning, driving kids with disabilities around in the golf cart, campfire setup and cleanup, night hike preparation—whatever Dad needed. We always brought in college kids as summer staff, and it was my job to show them the ropes: rules, first aid, care of the equipment, identifying poisonous plants and bugs. I don't mean to sound like a jerk here, but sometimes I'm amazed at how much some college kids don't know about the real world: the basic stuff like I just mentioned.

Reece was baby-sitting all summer; Mei would be helping her mom with catering. Skid was hush-hush about his plans. Rob's parents got lots of insurance money from the tornado damage and went gangbusters on fixing up The Castle. They were always asking his advice about styles and colors so he'd feel included. We didn't hang around there much—still being kind of embarrassed about that face-off with Uncle Dorian over the almost-divorce. But Rob said they were working things out, and that was good. After the week "getting down to the Get Down" at Farr Island, then the tornado nearly destroying his house, and then putting on the breastplate of righteousness and pulling his family back together, my cousin was a changed man.

On top of our separate duties, we had high school summer reading assignments. But for all of us, finding the armor of God was number one.

"Bloocifer's loose! Elijah, HELP!!" My little twin sisters came barreling down the hill straight toward us, yelling and panicky. "Bloocifer's loose!"

I dropped down off my perch, my mind instantly in camp crisis mode. "Did you tell Dad?"

Skid sat up uneasily. "Who's Bloocifer?"

I said to the girls, "Okay. Get to the house and tell Mom. And tell Reece and Mei to sit tight. Whatever you do, stay on the path. Now go!" They ran squealing up toward home. I took off for the nature center, the guys chasing along behind me. I answered Skid as we ran. "He's a blue racer—fast, aggressive."

Mentally I swept the camp. A bunch of preschoolers were bug hunting in the wildflower meadow next to Frog Lagoon; middle schoolers milled around their cabins on the other hill. I could hear kids at the pool behind the lodge. *Blue racers like water,* I cautioned myself.

"Bloocifer?" Skid asked worriedly. "You mean as in *Lucifer?*"

"Boo-Blue-Lucifer-Racer, all in one. Rob thought up the name. Racers move up to eight miles an hour and have vicious bites. Bloocifer hates humans—especially me. I'm the one who caught him. Watch your step—he could be anywhere."

Rob's eyes were glued to the ground as we ran. "I've seen him pushing the lid of his cage open, trying to escape. He raises his head like a cobra and darts back and forth. He's a maniac! If you see a six-foot streak of light blue-green in the grass, run like the wind!"

Skid sprinted alongside me. "I never heard of a blue racer."

"They're not real common," I explained. "Sort of Egyptian-looking eyes. A reptile expert from Cleveland drove all the way down here once to buy Bloocifer for a lot of money, but Dad wouldn't sell. People drop by the nature center all the time just to see him." We reached the door. "Let me go in first in case he's curled up in a corner."

Slowly, I opened the door and peeked into the entry hall. I dashed in and whirled around, checking above the door along the casing. *All clear, so far.* I approached the reptile room, keeping an eye on the fake oak tree in the corner; he could come dripping off the plastic limb that arched over the room, and I'd never know it. I listened. No sound. Not that I expected one. Chills slithered down my back, and I pulled my T-shirt tight around my neck.

The other reptiles were in their tanks and cages: garter snakes, lizards, an iguana, a snapping turtle. The lid to Bloocifer's cage was knocked a little off. What if the twins had been pretending he was a lobbie, one of their make-believe woodland creatures, and had tried to feed him some of their weed salad? But no, they were afraid of him. Everyone was. Even Bo kept his distance.

The front door down the hall behind me creaked open. "Okay in there?" came Skid's cautious voice.

"No sign of him yet," I called back quietly.

"Rob and I are coming in. Your dad's on his way."

"Okay, but slow and quiet."

They eased up behind me. I nodded at a door to the right. "Aquariums are in there." I nodded to the left, "Land animals are in there. Take your pick."

"Which way would he go?" Rob asked.

I gave him a look. "He didn't say."

Rob screwed his mouth up. "Well, you know weird nature stuff. I just figured—"

"That I know how snakes think?" I said.

Skid laughed.

I headed past the aquariums. "Actually, he's probably behind the freezer in the supply room. I'll check there first. That's where we keep the frozen mice, and snakes like the heat from the motor."

Rob said to Skid, "See what I mean? He *does* know how they think."

I was poking around under the freezer when I heard a gasp from the woodland room and dashed in.

Rob was peering into a cage. "Isn't this Lady Nibbler's?"

"Yeah, where is she?" The chipmunk's cage was empty. "Oh no," I groaned. "The twins are going to freak. She was their favorite."

Dad came in and bristled at the news that Bloocifer and Lady Nibbler were both missing. "This is not good. Nori and Stacy . . ." He sighed long and hard. "Let your mom break the news to them." He grunted in frustration. "We're going to have pandemonium if this gets out. How did he escape in the first place? Haven't I made Bloocifer's craftiness clear?" His head jerked; he looked at me. "Who was the last one in here?"

I shrugged innocently. "Beats me. But hey, Dad, you

could offer a reward. I even bet I know where he is!"

Dad shook his head. "No rewards. The place would be crawling with snake hunters."

"You're kidding!" Skid said.

Dad gave a chuckle. "Naturalists are a strange breed." He thought a minute. "We'll have to let the counselors know. Elijah, do a sweep of the vicinity, especially around the cabins and down by the lake. Take a burlap sack . . . and a hoe. I'd hate to kill him, but it's not likely we can take him alive a second time."

We went back outside, and I sprinted up to the porch where Reece and Mei were watching for us. I filled them in.

Reece made a yuck face. "You're actually going to catch him?"

"Sure, but it's not a one-man job. Skid and Rob are going to help."

Reece huffed at me. "I'm not missing the adventure!"

"Reece," I said tolerantly, "he's really fast."

She just laughed. "You could outrun him with a fellow freshman on your back, couldn't you?"

"Is it a poison snake?" Mei asked. She pulled a quartz crystal out of her pocket and squeezed it tight in her hand.

I guess I gave her a weird look, because she smiled like she was embarrassed and said, "It is for good luck—to keep away evil."

I said skeptically, "Okay . . ."

Dad closed the door behind us. "By the way, while you're

all together, do you kids know anything about campfires burning in Council Cliffs State Park after dark? Officer Taylor called and asked."

We all said no.

"Well, it's illegal," Dad said with a tone of warning.

It wasn't that my dad didn't trust me, even after all I'd put him through the last year. But I am, after all, the expert on fire at Camp Mudjokivi. And my clan did hang out in the far reaches of Owl Woods and beyond.

Skid said, "Rumor at school has it that satanists hang out in those hills."

Dad dismissed that with a chuckle. "I've heard the rumors. If you hear anything that makes *logical* sense, let me know. Hermits' Cave is not that far from camp."

The glance he gave us as he headed back to his office was like a warning shot: no more trouble, all right?

I armed everyone with broomsticks and took the hoe myself to pin Bloocifer down; if he attacked I'd have to hack him in two. I didn't really want Reece going, but she insisted. Half an hour later, we'd turned up zip, so we gathered back at the front porch.

Reece and Mei fixed a tea party for the twins to cheer them up about losing Lady Nibbler (who was most likely swallowed whole and working her way through Bloocifer's digestive system, but I kept that part to myself). While the tea party went on, Rob, Skid, and I headed back down to the gazebo near the lake, posting watch for Bloocifer and planning our first clan expedition to the cliffs. Rob stretched out on the bench again, his round eyes roaming the gazebo rafters. "You said he could be anywhere?"

Chapter 2

COUNCIL Cliffs State Park is a series of water-made sandstone gorges with cliffs, waterfalls, and shallow caves—unusual for this part of the country and the best-kept secret in the state as tourist attractions go.

Northern plant life like eastern hemlock, American beech, black birch, and all kinds of ferns live in the damp, shady gorges. But up on the rims of the gorges where it's drier and warmer, you'll find plant life more suited to dry southern climates. Dad takes older campers on nature hikes there, so I've been to each gorge more times than I can count. It's fun to go off by myself—like when Dad has me run ahead to plant clues for a nature scavenger hunt. Some old hermits used to live there, and I can see why they'd want to. The streams and pools are clear; there are plenty of grapevines to swing on and huge ledges to camp under where it's dry and sandy.

For our first search for the next piece of armor, Skid's mom drove us to Council Cave, the closest site to Magdeline's main road. Carlotta Skidmore had a huge book to read and a thermos of iced tea. "Take all the time you want, kids," she said as we got out of the car. "I have three hundred pages left." She reclined her car seat and rolled down the windows. "I'll get comfortable here."

We followed the wide, flat path with cliffs rising to our left and right. In fifteen minutes we reached the back of the canyon and stood under a huge, horseshoe-shaped ledge of red sandstone. A narrow waterfall poured over the cliff into a wide, sandy bowl in front of us. The air was cool and damp in the shade of the overhang.

"This is so beautiful! The air smells so clean!" Reece said. "Don't you feel like you're in Arizona or New Mexico? Mei, this is more like the Southwest."

"I'd like to see the Southwest," Mei said, gazing around with her mouth in a wide-open smile. "I'd like to see all of America."

"Me too," said Reece. "Someday we'll all go together!"

Mei took pictures of us goofing off, and then I said, "This is where we'll start searching for the next piece of the armor."

"Hey, guys," Reece said, "you know what I just thought of? There wasn't a clue with the breastplate of righteousness, was there? We had the piece of baby blanket with the helmet of salvation and the compass with the belt of truth. But there wasn't a third clue. I wonder why?"

Skid said, "Maybe that's the end of the Dowland story."

"That can't be the end," said Rob. "Dowland said, 'Piece by piece . . . *they* will rest in peace.' That has to mean all the pieces of the armor. And besides that, we still don't know who's in the reject grave. Dowland's mystery is not over."

Skid argued, "Does '*they* will rest in peace' refer to armor pieces or people?" He shrugged. "We don't know."

Reece shivered, "More dead people? I hope not! Hey, let's go wading, everybody!" She kicked off her sandals.

"It'll be cold," I warned, but she didn't listen.

Mei followed Reece knee-deep into the pool, singing, "I love American school, I love American school!"

Rob sat on a log and studied his maps. "School's out."

"That's what I mean!" she yelled over the noisy falls. "In Japan we go to school in June and July. And we have cram school in the afternoons to prepare for college exams. Only August is for vacation. But in America no school in June and July! When I am a junior, I will get my license here. In Japan it costs thousands of dollars to get a license!"

"You mean to buy a car," Rob corrected.

"No, to get a driver's license. Over $2,000!" She added cheerily, "My mother is getting her license this week because it's so cheap here. She can drive us places!"

"Come wading, guys!" Reece coaxed us.

"Your mom doesn't have a driver's license!?" Rob asked Mei.

Skid was sunning himself on a rock like a skinny black cat. He added his two cents. "In Japan everyone rides trains and buses as much as cars. It's like Europe—you can go anywhere anytime. The speed trains are awesome! At a hundred-and-seventy miles an hour, they're the classiest land transit in the world."

I sat on Skid's rock and untied my shoes.

Mei added, "It's called *Shinkansen* in Japan. You should

ride it sometime!" Then she burst into a singsong voice and danced around in the water with her arms thrown out. "And guess what? My father is staying longer in America!"

Skid caught my eye, tipped his head knowingly toward Mei, and mouthed the words, "The butterfly emerges."

No sooner had I waded in than Reece limped out. "My toes are freezing!"

"Told you," I teased. "If you wade in wintertime, it'll give you an ice cream headache. No joke, I've done it."

"Let's get on with it, Creek," Skid said impatiently, "while we're still young. What's the plan?"

I scooped a handful of water and whipped it in his direction, soaking his midsection. He rolled off the rock. "That's it, Creek. You've had it!"

He took off after me like a bolt of black lightning. But I had three advantages: no shoes, a head start, and the cliff. Tearing straight through the big, sandy pool where Skid wouldn't follow in his expensive high-tops, I scrambled up some boulders. I ignored Reece when she yelled for me to get my crazy self down and scooted along the edge, my back pressed into the rock until I'd made it to a hole thirty feet above the floor of the gorge. I stood at the edge and grinned down at Skid. There was no way he'd try that ledge, not with his fear of heights—which was my fourth advantage.

He sized up the cliff and yelled threateningly over the waterfall, "Creek, you're running up a tab! One day soon

I'm collecting!" He paced under me like a hungry panther. "Don't think I won't. When you least expect it . . ."

The girls nagged me down, and we found a quiet place in the sun away from the noise and sightseers who'd started filing through. Even as things settled, I kept Skid in my field of vision. Reece sat down slowly and rubbed her knee.

"What's wrong?" I asked.

"Just the cold. It aches. It'll be fine. What's our next plan of action?"

"Resume speed!" Mei chirped. She was nuts about learning driving vocab.

Rob pointed out on the map the different sites in the park: "We're here at Council Cave; there's Hermits' Cave— that's the site you can see from Telanoo. Eagle Rock Falls connects with Hermits' Cave. East of that is Cathedral Cave. We should scout one section at a time."

"Let's start with a sweep of the gorge," I suggested. "There's a trail up there too." I pointed to the rim of the canyon and said to Reece encouragingly, "We'll get it on another day. It's not a huge climb, and the view is really great."

Reece said, "Read about the next piece, Skid."

He looked up the Ephesians passage in the Quella. "Next we have to find shoes. It says, 'with your feet fitted with the readiness that comes from the gospel of peace.'"

Rob asked, "Which means . . . shoes of . . . the what?"

Skid said, "Yeah, this was a tough one, so I checked the footnote. It said that shoes are the most underrated piece of military equipment. Without good shoes soldiers can lose their footholds over steep terrain. Without sturdy soles men get tired more easily, can't run fast, or stand their ground in the heat of battle."

"Women too!" Reece said.

"Okay, Elliston. No offense intended. The footnote says these shoes of peace are a paradox. Why does the Bible say we should wear shoes of *peace* into spiritual *war?* Seems like a contradiction. But it means that when you're ready to fight for God, you bring peace to people. Peace inside." He pocketed the Quella. "That's all I got."

Mei dried off her feet with a handkerchief. "I don't understand about the war you are talking about. In Japan we don't like war."

Reece said, "It's not war with guns. It's war like . . . like when Rob stood up against his dad. He was fighting for peace in his family."

Mei nodded and frowned at the same time. "It's very difficult."

Rob rolled his eyes in agreement. "It was! I was shaking like a leaf."

Skid looked around at the gorge. "So where will this paradox pair be? Anybody got a bright idea?"

Fighting off a hollow feeling, I glanced around the vast span of cliff above our heads, then down the gorge trail with its acres of sloping banks on each side. "So far the other pieces were in the opposite environment: helmet of salvation in a dead church graveyard and belt of truth pointing to a lie. The breastplate of righteousness was in a place Dowland considered evil. So . . . what's opposite of the 'readiness that comes from the gospel of peace'?"

"Well, *gospel* means 'good news,'" Reece explained.

Rob answered, "Then it must mean the *un*readiness of the *bad* news of *war.*"

Skid retorted sarcastically, "Thanks for clearing that up, Wingate. Now we can move ahead."

In the cool shade of the cliff, we sat thinking. Misty sunbeams filtered down through the high trees of the upper rim, turning the pool to amber. A family with three little kids was wading, taking turns sticking their heads under the falls. They laughed and splashed, all golden and peaceful, as we watched from the shadows. I knew some of the history of the place, and it was hard to believe that we were in . . .

"Oh wow!" I said with a sudden sense of awe. "Do you know where we are right now?"

Mei said, "Council Cliffs State Park!"

"Exactly. And do you know what used to happen here?" I asked, chills running down my back.

Rob's jaw dropped. "Yeah! Indian councils."

I nodded mysteriously. "War councils. To discuss war."

"To get ready," Reece added eerily, "for the bad news of war. The shoes are here—they have to be! Awesome!"

Mei looked around hopelessly. "But this is a very big place."

"Yeah, and more bad news," I said. "This is the smallest of all the sites! We'd better hope they're here, or this could take all summer."

"I'm game!" Mei said, sticking her hand out. "Every day with my friends *all summer!* A cord of five strands is not quickly broken."

We piled our hands on Mei's and repeated the cord-of-five-strands line.

Rob rolled up his maps and checked the skies. "It's clouding up. Now that we know this is the place, we might find new clues in Dowland's journals about where the treasure is buried. His scrawls could lead us to the exact spot."

"Let's do it," Skid said, jumping up. "To the police station, my people!"

We made our way back through the gorge. Reece hung back and curled her finger at me when I turned to wait for her. She whispered, "Elijah, I want to do a real group ceremony sometime like you said. Forming an official clan or tribe or whatever is a good idea."

"Okay," I said and turned to go on.

She grabbed my shirt, holding me back while the others went ahead. "I mean it. It's for Mei," she whispered, "so she'll really feel like a part of the quest."

"She doesn't?" I asked.

Reece looked worried. "I don't know. A couple of days ago she hinted about how she liked helping us, but that we could get along okay without her."

"She seemed fine today."

"I know," Reece said, but her worried look stayed.

Chapter 3

꙳꙳

SKID'S mom dropped us off at the police station.

Reece led the way to the front desk. "Hi, we're the kids who were working on the Dowland case. We'd like to see the journals, please."

The lady officer gave us a doubtful look.

Reece said, "We're helping Officer Taylor close the case. You can ask him."

"Just a moment," she said.

"Just ask Officer Taylor," Reece called after her. "Tell him it's Elijah and Reece and—"

The door slammed.

In a moment Officer Taylor came out with a curious expression. He was in uniform as always, with a straight back and an official look. His kind face and good sense of humor made him the favorite policeman at our school. The kids always wanted him to do the safety and drug speeches. "Hi, kids, what do you need?"

"The journals," said Reece with a big smile.

He gave us an odd look. "Your friend picked them up already."

"What friend?" Skid asked.

"That doctor who did the scientific tests for you."

"Dr. Stallard?!" Reece asked.

A jolt of electricity went through me.

Officer Taylor saw our confused expressions. "That's what it said in the file. Aren't you working with the Stallards to find that old suit of armor?"

"Yes, but they weren't supposed to take the journals," Reece said. "They didn't ask us or say anything about it."

Officer Taylor looked puzzled. "Let me check on something." He went into the back room.

I looked at Skid. "Did *you* say they could—"

He put up his hands. "I don't know a thing."

In a minute Officer Taylor came back, flipping through a file folder. "Here's the note that says you kids could look at the journals and . . . information about the forensic tests done by the Stallards. One of our dispatchers apparently signed the journals out to Dr. Stallard a few days ago."

"Maybe they just wanted a quick look," I said hopefully, but a gritty feeling had already settled into my chest.

Rob spoke up. "The Stallards left weeks ago. They're back in Chicago."

I asked Officer Taylor, "Did they say when they'd bring the journals back?"

He flipped through the papers in the file. "It doesn't say. It's not critical that we have them back immediately. The detective has gone through the journals and didn't find anything useful."

"But we need them!" Rob cried.

Officer Taylor frowned. "I'm sorry. All I have here is a

note that they were checked out. I can ask the dispatcher when she comes in."

We'd just stepped outside when clouds burst and rain fell in buckets.

Skid turned and faced me. "Don't panic."

"Right," I said. "Skid, if your mom asks, say the Stallards have the journals for a while and leave it at that. No freaking out until we get their side of the story."

I knew if we went back to camp for a powwow, the college staff would be twisting my arm to lead some dumb indoor games or give a nature lecture to a pack of wet, fidgety campers, and I wasn't in the mood. We hashed out our options and ended up at The Castle. Everyone ran squalling toward the house like they were being bombed. I took my time. (I've never understood why people run to get out of the rain. It's just water.) The saggy front porch of The Castle had been ripped out, so we had to circle around heaps of raggedy carpet and scrap wood to get through the backyard.

"Renovation," Rob said while we dripped off in the kitchen.

Brand-new windows in an old style were going in. The matted carpet was gone, and the old wood floors were being shined up. Furniture in the living room was shoved into the corner and covered with drop cloths.

Aunt Grace bubbled all over us. "We're getting fresh

paint in vintage hues throughout! And guess what? We found a false wall, which is coming out in a few weeks. The space may be big enough for a walk-in closet in one of the guest rooms!"

Uncle Dorian was busy stripping wallpaper. He wouldn't make eye contact with us. We climbed two flights to the leaky attic and sat in a circle, using crates and what was left of the Victorian couch the tornado had torn up. The attic was pretty much a wreck, and the surviving mannequins were a sorry bunch, piled in the corner with missing heads and arms and hair.

Our suspicions about the Stallards came boiling out.

"I'm calling them now!" I yelled. "I'll demand to have the journals back. They had no right to take them!"

"Hold your fire," Skid said. "Let me see what's up. Not a good idea to let them know that we know. I'll ask for an update on the breastplate of righteousness and see if they say anything."

Rob puffed out his chest proudly. "You can use my phone. I have one in my room now."

In ten minutes Skid came sauntering back up the stairs, his expression cold as stone. "She denied it."

I jumped to my feet. "What?! How could they lie to us like that?"

Skid said, "I wasn't going to mention the journals, but when Dr. Eloise said that they're ready to deliver the breastplate, I said, 'Great, and maybe we'll talk about the journals when you come.' She said 'Fine,' and that she was excited to see the rest of them. Didn't even throw me a crumb."

"We know where their office is," I said with threat in my voice. "We could get Reece's mom to drive us back up to Chicago and, you know—"

"Don't say break in, Elijah Creek!" Reece snapped.

"Wait, hear me out. We could show up one day, and while one of us distracts them, the rest could be looking around."

Rob argued, "They wouldn't have Dowland's journals just lying around! They'd be in a vault or down in that museum crypt. We should invite them down here and have them arrested for stealing evidence!"

"Mei, what's wrong?" Reece asked.

Mei was staring down at the floor, stiff and frightened. Her happy, dancing-in-the-pool mood was gone. "Maybe I should go home."

Reece said, "It's okay, Mei. We didn't do anything wrong. It'll be okay."

"I know," she said and paused a long time, still staring at the floor. Finally she said, "My parents are worried about me. They are a little bit . . . suspicious . . . about what we are doing."

Skid put his arm around Mei. "Chill, Aizawa. We'll get it straight and probably get medals of honor for helping the police. Piece of cake, easy as pie."

Remembering how Mei had started keeping a crystal to ward off evil, I said confidently, "You're safe with us."

Reece said cheerfully, "Hey, I know! Before we confront the Stallards, I'll have Mom call Officer Taylor, and he can ask the dispatcher to give a description of the person who took the journals!"

"Too many people involved," I worried out loud. "We should work directly with the police."

"No more police!" Mei cried. "My parents think I'm in trouble!"

Rob tried to console her. "It seems like some deep, dark mystery. I mean, it *is* a mystery. But we're not in any danger or trouble. Dowland's dead and so is his dog. Theobald's cooling off. We're not hiding anything from our parents. I mean, they don't really believe it's the armor of God anyway. At least mine don't."

Mei said, "I . . . maybe you should go . . . without me."

I glanced over at Reece and saw more worry.

We left the whole subject of the stolen journals and went to how people like to solve mysteries and how it's no big deal because almost everyone in the world has a deep, dark secret to hide. Then Reece said, "I have an idea. Let's each share our deepest, darkest secret."

"You start, Reece," Skid said. "You're the mouth of the bunch."

"And you're the ears, so listen up." She sat back and thought for a while. "This is kind of hard . . . well, I haven't told anyone, but my bone condition is not getting better. Surgery should have fixed it, but it didn't." She half grinned as if it were no big deal. "It's not really a secret, I guess. I'm still using crutches and canes. That's it, that's my secret. Okay, Mei, your turn—your deepest, darkest secret."

"I don't know," she said. We waited but she just got flustered. "I can't think of one."

Reece said, "That's okay. You can think about it awhile. Rob, what's yours?"

I was glad she called on him next because I didn't know what to say. I had one, but I couldn't let the cat out of the bag. Rob tried to pass, but Reece wouldn't let him. "Come on, pleeeeeze!"

"Well . . . okay . . . but you can't laugh."

Skid snickered. "Wouldn't think of it."

Rob bit his lip. "Here's something nobody knows because I just decided it: I know what I want to be when I grow up."

"Really? What?" Reece asked eagerly.

He turned pink and mumbled, "A storm chaser."

You could have knocked me over with a feather. *Scaredy-cat Rob? My bookworm cousin? A storm chaser?*

"What is a storm chaser?" Mei asked.

Rob answered, "A weatherman who chases tornadoes around the countryside to find out how they work."

Mei said. "Chasing tornadoes? It sounds dangerous!"

Reece laughed in disbelief. "It's very dangerous!"

Rob said defensively, "I know. But I've been reading up on it."

Skid calmly said, "Makes sense, Wingate, what with the maps and charts and figuring things out like you do. Good call."

I thought about our run-in with the tornado, how it all worked to bring his family back together. "I can sort of see you doing that, I guess."

We gave him a little grief, but it was cool to see my cousin keep changing like that right before my eyes.

"How about you, Skid?" Reece asked.

He squirmed uncomfortably on his crate, then got a faraway look. It took him a minute. I could tell he wasn't sure whether to trust us or not. We egged him on. Finally he said, "Okay. I . . . uh . . . I lost a year."

"What do you mean?" Reece asked.

"I'm a year older than you guys."

For some weird reason that gave me a kick, realizing that he was cooler than us partly just because he was older. In an instant I was trying to measure how cool he was six months ago, and if in six months I might measure up to that. Dumb, but there you have it.

He explained, "When my parents split up, I went on the lam, flunked most of my classes."

Skid flunked!? Mr. Teacher's Pet Student of the Year flunked?

"So, Wingate," he said, "that's why I was impressed by how you handled yourself last spring. You were seriously messed up—no question about it—but you kept on plugging; you stayed in the game. That's it: my deep, dark secret. You can tell anyone, I don't care."

Reece said, "There's no need to. Clan secret." She smiled at Mei.

"Your turn, Creek," Skid said. "Deepest, darkest."

"I don't really have any . . ."

"Come on," said Rob.

"Really, I don't, not one that I can talk about yet."

"Not fair!" Reece said.

"Bet I know," Skid smirked. For a guy who kept his status with Miranda Varner highly classified, I'd have thought he'd steer clear of the subject of Reece and me. I shot him a look, and it must have been a pretty deadly one. His eyebrows went up and his head shot back. "Just kidding, man. We're cool."

If he'd said one word, he'd have been as sorry-looking as the mannequins. "I need to think about it," I said, "like Mei. We'll tell ours later, won't we, Mei?"

Mei nodded at the floor.

Reece switched subjects again, plainly trying to keep Mei happy. "Okay then, back to the Stallards. We don't need the journals to get started searching for the shoes of peace. I think we should tell Officer Taylor what we found out, though. I'll pass the word along."

"Not yet," I said.

"Why not?" Reece asked. "We can trust Officer Taylor."

Skid agreed with me. "Let's talk to the Stallards face-to-face. In the meantime we'll start taking each site of Council Cliffs one at a time like Elijah said."

To keep the peace, Reece agreed. She squeezed Mei's hand. "We can have picnics and take our summer books to read. Just the five of us together! Nature walks and wading. It'll be fun!" She stood and grimaced in pain. "Hey, Rob, I want to see the rest of your house. Come on, Mei. I bet it's going to be the prettiest house in Magdeline."

Heading down the attic stairs, I said to Rob, "I'm going to miss the rats in the walls and the drippy roof in the attic. It won't be the same."

"I'll live with it," he said back.

"By the way," I added, "I could use that scrap wood in the backyard."

"You and your fires, Creek," Skid said sarcastically.

"It's not for a fire."

I did have a deep, dark secret, but I wasn't giving any hints—not yet.

Chapter 4

THE roar and clunk of heavy equipment woke me at the crack of dawn. I sat up and looked out my window. It was just past 6:30, and somebody was bulldozing Old Pilgrim Church! After the winter and the tornado cleanup, it was finally happening! I yanked on shorts and a T-shirt and ran out the back door. Halfway across the yard, I stopped. Bumping along on his dozer was Theobald!

I backed up and cut around to the front door of the lodge. From the main room, I'd be able to watch through the window and not be seen. I wanted to call the others— this was important—but it was too early. They'd still be asleep.

A pang went through my heart as I stood there alone, watching a truck of fill dirt pull in and the old church go under for the last time. I knew it wasn't really a church— just a building like Reece said—but I still felt sad. It had been there long before there'd ever been a Camp Mudj. It was Dowland's dream to have a big church, and that was never going to happen. I felt sorry for him and even sorrier about the dead church.

Magdeline wasn't really keen on churches, I guess. We had a couple outside the city limits and in the next towns, like Reece's church. But in town we had only one church group left: the Blessed Assembly of the Full Gospel of the Holy Ghost. They meet in what used to be Eibeck's Tavern and which still leans to the trashy side, looks-wise. Another group abandoned their church building on Paris Street. It was now Anne Wasserman's Foggiest Notions antique shop. That was it for churches.

I'd never been curious about churches, but I was now.

More dump trucks emptied their loads, and by lunchtime the old ruin became a future garden or volleyball court. It was ironic to me that Theobald, who'd been a suspect in Kate Dowland's death and had a part in destroying her father's church, was burying it for good.

I got busy with camp stuff until a flatbed truck came hauling a backhoe. Theobald unloaded it and headed around the back of the graveyard to the lonely plot outside the fence.

Then the police showed up. My heart jumped into my throat. *Calm down,* I told myself. *You're not in trouble. We'll finally know who died and maybe how.*

I ran to the camp office to use the phone and gave the same message four times: "Get over here! They're digging up the reject grave!"

Reece, Mei, and Rob got rides. Skid wasn't home. Still leery of Theobald, we hid out in the lodge until he hopped off the backhoe and drove away. The last of the digging was done by hand.

A short, stocky guy with a shovel dropped down into the

hole. In a few minutes, his head disappeared, but wads of dirt kept flying out of the grave. We figured he was close, but he kept on digging, deeper and deeper. We eased out of the lodge and stood there by the pool fence, watching.

"It's Dowland's wife, I bet," I said, nervous and excited.

Reece agreed. "The only thing that makes sense. The stone doesn't look that old. And he was the only one around there for years."

"I bet he killed her over the armor," Rob said.

The digger tossed his shovel up out of the hole and climbed out.

"They found her!" I said.

A man I figured to be a detective was looking into the hole and talking to the gravedigger. Nothing happened for a while. We walked over. "Hey, what'd you find in there?" I asked.

Irritated, the gravedigger wiped his brow. "Nothing."

"There's no body down there?!" I asked.

"Nope." He went back to the hole muttering, "Seven feet down . . . nothing."

We looked at each other. We went over and looked down into the hole. A guilty feeling crept over me. *All that trouble for nothing . . .*

I said to the detective, "We thought for sure—"

Reece jumped in, "There was a headstone and no body? What kind of sense does that make?"

He made a note in his little book, then gave us a

disapproving glance. "You're the kids in the middle of this investigation?"

"Yes, sir," I said.

"Thanks for your help, but we can take it from here."

"We thought it would be Mrs. Dowland," I said sincerely. "She died, but Rob didn't find any notice of it in the town records. We thought that Mr. Dowland buried her here."

Ignoring me, the detective strolled over to the gravedigger to talk business.

I felt like yesterday's news.

Rob said quietly, "No journals, no body."

I said, "No shoes, no clues."

"No problem," Reece said cheerfully.

Whatever made that girl tick, I wanted some of it.

On the way back to my house, Reece spewed out her thoughts. "Okay, then Mrs. Dowland—or some clue related to her—must be buried with the shoes of peace. Maybe they're not in the park after all. Sure, the bad news of war may describe Council Cliffs, but we have to remember that Dowland buried the pieces related to his own personal opinions."

Rob said, "The place of war in Dowland's mind wouldn't be Council Cave. It would be where big fights broke out, where all the trouble was . . ."

Our eyes drifted over to the plot of packed dirt that used to be Old Pilgrim Church.

"It wasn't there," I said.

"You're sure?" Reece asked.

"Sure," I said as another gritty feeling crept into my chest. "I checked it out."

Reece turned to Rob. "Okay, maybe the big fights were with his wife. If we can find where she's really buried—"

Rob said mysteriously, "The old newspapers only talked about the daughter going to Ireland to study. No one knew at the time that she died in the well. But the wife isn't mentioned. She just dropped out of sight." He nodded toward the open grave. "Maybe he buried her there and then dug her up, like he did the armor."

"Gross!" Reece cried. "That is so—" she turned to Mei, "How do you say it in Japanese?"

"*Kimoi,*" Mei answered, distracted. "Are there . . . other old wells in town?"

We got quiet. "Probably," Rob said. "Probably a lot of them."

"You're not saying . . ." I gulped. "We'd have to fine-tooth comb the entire county! That could take years. I'd be a Really Old Man Eating Out by then!"

"You as an old man? *Kimoi* again!" said Reece, grinning at me.

I said, "It's fine to do some checking, but I think we should start at Council Cliffs where the raven flew. That looked like a sign to me."

Skid sailed in on his board. Reece filled him in, but he was only half listening, and with the strangest look on his face. I interrupted Reece. "What's up?"

"I got to thinking last night about how Dowland liked to play around with opposites. He said his daughter left town when actually she died. So it follows that he'd say his wife died—"

"When she actually left town!" Reece cried.

"Yeah, but here's where it gets weird. I've been talking to Charlie at Florence's. I asked him to tell me everything he remembered about Mrs. Dowland from all those years ago."

"And?" Reece said.

"He said she was small and slim, brown curly hair. Knew a lot about the Bible—more than her husband even. Nervous type. A fancy talker, he called her." He paused, then said dramatically, "Does that sound like anyone you know?"

Rob wheezed, "Noooooo! Are you saying that Dr. Eloise is *Stan Dowland's wife?!*"

We went all to pieces, gasping and gaping at each other in shock. Reece looked horrified. "That's exactly how the dispatcher described the journal thief: small, slim, nervous, with curly hair!"

I glared at her. "You weren't supposed to talk about it with the police! We agreed!"

She glared back. "I didn't! Officer Taylor asked the dispatcher, then told my mom, and she told me."

"I said before, that's too many people involved!" I barked. "And why didn't you tell us this?"

"I knew you'd be mad, that's why! I just found out, and anyway, forget about the people involved. The point is that

Dowland's ex-wife *is* Dr. Eloise *is* the journal thief!"

Rob took off on a tirade. "Oh, I see it. I see it all now. A perfect fit! The church closes, her daughter dies, her life falls apart. She leaves but still wants to have the armor of God, to know its secrets. But Stan Dowland buries it to keep her from finding it. She marries an archaeologist to help her with the quest. And now she's wormed her way into our lives!"

"That's what I was thinking," Skid said. "But there's a problem. She made friends with my family *before* we moved to Magdeline. We met in the Middle East, remember?"

"Freak coincidence! It happens all the time," Rob said.

Reece came back with, "It doesn't happen all the time, Rob. That's why they're called *freak* coincidences!"

I jumped in. "What about those old pictures on their office wall? She and Dale have been married for decades."

"And Dowland's wife left decades ago. I still say it fits," Rob snipped.

"She did say she had a fake name," I recalled.

Reece argued, "But that was to protect them when they worked in The Window, a dangerous part of the world for missionaries."

"Likely story," Rob said. "They've never come right out and said they were missionaries. They just led us to believe that's why they used fake names!"

"She has the journals," I said angrily, "and I bet she can get into Dowland's house!"

Reece asked, "I don't get why she waited months after Dowland died to get the journals. Why not step up, say she was his wife, and—"

"To avoid the questioning about Kate Dowland and that whole mess," I said.

"This is unbelievable!" Reece cried.

Mei didn't say a word the whole time. Not a peep.

"That's not the end of it," Skid said. "I got a call from the Stallards this morning. They're ready to deliver the breastplate of righteousness. Tomorrow."

Chapter 5

AUNT Grace and Uncle Dorian finished decorating the first floor only hours before the Stallards came with the breastplate of righteousness. We had to sort of dress up. I wore my one white shirt. We waited in "the parlor," which had been called the living room before all the decorating.

"The Stallards are Mom's first high tea guinea pigs," whispered Rob. He loosened his collar with his finger. "If it goes good, the famous scientists can take our brochures about the Wingate Bed and Breakfast and Tea Room all the way back to Chicago."

"What if it flops?" I teased.

I figured he'd pop me, but he grinned. "If it flops," he said straightening his tie, "then they're just a couple of wacky out-of-towners, what do they know, and we keep the brochures."

Reece snipped, "Brochures?! Why are we talking about brochures? I think we should have them arrested on the spot. Did she think we're idiots? Did she think we'd never figure it out?"

Usually the cool one, Skid roamed the parlor, peeking through the curtains every few seconds and muttering to himself, "If this is a con . . . if this is a cold-blooded, dirty-dealin' con . . ." Suddenly he flipped the curtain closed. "Here they come. Play 'em, now; don't let 'em play us."

Reece said, "This is confusing! I don't know who I'm talking to. Mei, you sit by me, okay?"

I half whispered, "She's Dr. Eloise until further notice. Stan Dowland's ex-wife is not going to blow her cover until she gets what she's looking for: the whole armor of God."

The Stallards came in hauling a big box, but before we could have a look at the armor piece, Aunt Grace floated by in her long dress and gloves, greeted us like we were total strangers, and made us sit at little tables. Then she floated out and back in again with pots of flavored tea and silver trays of cakes and sandwiches. Quiet music came on. Reece and Mei and Dr. Eloise thought it was the greatest thing ever. Dr. Dale played along; even Skid and Rob sat up straight with their hands in their laps. It was a little much for me.

"Good news," said Dr. Dale. "We have discovered a clue within a tiny pocket of the breastplate." He pulled out a scrap of yellowed paper. "It's a phone number, found in our last examination. Had we not detected the newer stitching along one of the seams, we never would have found it."

"The missing clue! Hey, Reece, the missing clue!" Rob cheered. "Whose phone number is it?"

"It belonged to a Brian Clarkson from Louisville, Kentucky. We've called him, and he seems to know nothing of Magdeline, Ohio, or Old Pilgrim Church. We didn't mention the armor, of course—only that we'd found this number in the effects of a deceased man, Stan Dowland. He'd never heard the name."

"It's a dead end?" Rob asked.

"Hardly," said Dr. Eloise, pointing up at nothing. "You see, this Mr. Clarkson moved to Louisville a few years ago."

I said flatly, "I don't get it."

She held up the paper. "Yellowed . . ."

Rob blurted out, "Previous owner? The phone number belonged to someone else a long time ago . . . like Dowland's wife, or . . ." He eyed her suspiciously. "Someone like *that.*"

Dr. Eloise tipped her head back. "Ah! Ah, so clever . . . We'll have to watch ourselves, Dale. These children are very quick."

I steamed.

Dr. Dale said, "We'll begin immediately to track down its original owner."

"The police could help. We're good friends with Officer Taylor," Skid said coolly, watching them for a reaction.

Aunt Grace floated in and out again. The Stallards gushed all over the puny sandwiches with no crusts and ignored the remark about the police.

When she left again, Dr. Eloise asked, "Marcus, you mentioned the journals in your call. What did you want to discuss?"

Skid said casually, "Oh, we went to get them, but they're checked out right now. We don't know who has them, but a lot of people are interested in the case, and we've been too busy to get back to the station on it."

I sized up their reactions. They just went on like it was no big deal.

Dr. Dale said, "The shoes, when you find them, may say *pax* or *paz*—Latin or Spanish for 'peace.' According to the fragments of legendary information we've collected, the sandals may have been in the possession of the apostle Paul, the first-century missionary to Europe and the Middle East. Later they may have gone to Eastern Europe or more likely into the hands of a certain Cabeza de Vaca, who was shipwrecked along the coast of America, although the names Wesley and certain tribal African names pop up in the armor legends. It's all very sketchy. If the original shoes wore out—which is a distinct possibility—new shoes may have been made from fresh materials and usable fragments of the old. Remember that the armor of God has been circling the globe for millennia, passing through many hands."

Dr. Eloise looked around at all of us sitting there stiff and formal and eyeballing her suspiciously. She suddenly asked, "Is everything all right, children?"

"Fine," I said coolly.

An awkward quiet settled over the room. The Stallards obviously didn't believe me.

Sloshing with tea and tired of the masquerade, I stood up. "I want to try on the vest."

As Dr. Eloise carefully fitted it on me, Dr. Dale pointed out which pieces of leather came from nearly thirty-five hundred years ago. "These are the exact types of skins used for the roof of the tabernacle. All three the same age and type. Fantastic, isn't it?"

Everybody closed in on me and started touching the vest, oohing and wowing. Dr. Eloise preached right in my face, "Once you have buckled on the omen belt and put on righteousness—the *gi*—prepare to find peace, Elijah Creek! *Y'shua Meshiach!*"

I was creeped out. This was a woman I thought was a scientist, then a dead woman, and now a live fake person who was going to let us find the armor of God and then snatch it out of our hands. I still couldn't understand, though, why she took the journals and signed her name. She could have borrowed them outright when the Dowland case closed. My mind was a mess.

I must have been showing the strain and chaos on my face; Reece smiled up at me, patted the vest, and whispered, "Perfect fit. Like it was made for you."

While Aunt Grace was in the kitchen, Dr. Eloise gathered us in a circle. "Now, if word ever reached the archaeology world about the near certainty of these tabernacle fragments, we'd be swarmed, swamped, inundated."

Dr. Dale nodded. "We've done all our testing in secret."

"Why?" Rob asked. "Why is an old tent cover so valuable?"

Dr. Eloise smiled warmly. "Excellent question, difficult answer. It's very odd to us that our nonbelieving colleagues find the ancient worship of the holy one so captivating. For them it's all about the rarity of artifacts. I wonder why one wants to enter the holy places and leave his heart at the door. The true value of discovery lies in experiencing the Presence."

I ran my hands over the leather, warm and smooth, and felt the cool metal brads that symbolized Jesus' death wounds. I put my finger in the little pocket under the brads that made the spear wound in his side, the pocket where the phone number had been hidden. Above the soft music and chatter came a cloudy quiet, almost like I was under water. It felt the same as when the voice told me to find the armor and later to watch for signs, but there were no words this time, more like a feeling of someone opening a door, a faraway life pulling at me. I wanted to follow, but to where I couldn't say.

I wondered what would happen when I had the whole armor on with the shoes on my feet and the shield and sword in my hands.

When I came back to the present, Skid and Reece were trading troubled glances, and I could tell just by the look in their eyes what they were thinking: they were wondering how Dr. Eloise or Mrs. Dowland could talk about God like he was the greatest thing ever, after living under an alias and stealing journals from a police department like a common thief.

"Have you begun to look for the next piece?" Dr. Eloise asked me directly.

Skid butted in, his voice cold, "We'll stay in touch."

"What omens are directing you?" she asked, eyeing us curiously.

"Omens?" Reece asked.

"As in 'truth,' dear. Remember *amen* and *omen* mean 'truth.' What truths are you following?"

"A little bird told me something," I said hesitantly.

Her face lit up. "Really?! Not in a deep gorge with a brook, I suppose?"

A chill went through me; she'd hit the nail on the head. "Um, sort of."

"Just like Elijah of old. Where? Where?" she asked hungrily.

"State park," I said, being vague. Skid scowled at me.

She glanced at Dr. Dale knowingly. "It's as we discussed. The park."

My heart skipped a beat. How did she know about that? Had they been following us? Were they trying to get ahead of us with their know-how and the journals?

She saw the shock on our faces, and her eyebrows went up. "Oh, we've been working, dears. After a series of wild goose chases, we found the faintest evidence that the shoes had a Moravian connection."

"What's that?" Rob asked.

"Another pot of tea, shall we? But brace yourselves. This story will leave you queasy."

Chapter 6

THEY took turns telling the tale, with Dr. Eloise throwing in the goriest parts and me getting more perturbed by the minute at her fake sincerity. "The year was 1775, children," Dr. Dale began, "and our nation was in the throes of childbirth. A band of Christians from Moravia had made the long, treacherous voyage to America to carry the good news of Jesus. They worked among the peaceful Lenape tribe—now known as the Delawares because they once lived along the Delaware River. In a short time, many of the Delawares moved to this area and came to a saving faith. Even one of the greatest war chiefs, Glikhican, determined to war no more. The believers established a town—Friedenstadt, meaning 'village of peace.'"

Dr. Eloise said, "Now, boys, I see you slumping in disappointment that an Indian war chief would settle down in a village of peace. But think about what peace meant: it meant comfortable homes, plenty of good food on the table, children having their fathers at home and not slaughtered and left to rot on a bloody battlefield. In the villages of peace, children like you no longer were awakened by blood-curdling screams and brutal attacks. At least, that was their hope." She smiled and patted my knee. "War sounds exciting, doesn't it? But live in the devastation and deprivation of it, and you see the truth: suffering families, foul water, scarce food . . . ," she paused and seemed to be reminiscing, "listening for the whine of bombs dropping, the screams of terror and pain . . . but I digress. Go on, Dale."

"There was not a tribe in Ohio who had not heard of the peace and success of the Moravian Delawares. But they still had enemies. Pagan Delawares were angry because their brothers had made friends with the white man. Some whites hated them simply because they were Indians. Others wanted their land. The British were determined to keep their claim on the New World. The Americans were fighting to gain their own country."

Dr. Eloise broke in sadly, "The peace and prosperity of one group often breeds envy and hatred in another. The British forced Glikhican and his people to uproot, leaving behind their homes and fields of corn. Their animals were shot. There was no food. It was a horrible, horrible time—a freezing winter in which babies died in their mothers' arms. Children, the shadowy steps of the evil one are never far behind those who walk the path of peace.

"A Colonel Williamson of the American forces was given free reign by his superiors to deal with Delaware Indians in any way he chose; he chose the worst kind of deception and cruelty. He met Glikhican's people in the fields with smiles and handshakes as they gathered what corn remained. But it was a trap, a terrible trap. One hundred of them were divided—the men from the women—and herded into rooms. Terrified, they were bound hand and foot all night. Amid tears and the horror of the unknown, Glikhican encouraged them to meet their fate with calm assurance that they would soon be in Heaven. The next morning they were executed, one by one their skulls crushed. Only two survived: one boy who hid beneath blood-soaked floorboards as his loved ones were being slaughtered, and another who was scalped and left for dead under a pile of corpses."

Seeing Reece's and Mei's appalled expressions, Dr. Dale broke in. "Perhaps a touch too many details, dearest. Have another cup. By March of 1782, seven short years later, the cities of peace were no more. The story of the massacre spread. So outraged were the other Delawares, so convinced that this was the true nature of the white man, that they resolved to obliterate them. A cancer of hate and fear grew, people killing people, Indian and white man, woman and child.

"So many times the beginnings of peace in Christian communities are haunted by shadowy steps of misunderstanding and prejudice. It's ever a struggle; evil presses in. But this is important to know: God is the prince of peace; he is also a man of war. There is no contradiction there— you will learn that later. Simply put, he will not let evil win."

"What happened to the two boys?" I asked.

"I knew you'd ask," Dr. Dale said with a smile. "You can understand the boys' mistrust of everyone: unbelieving

Delaware Indians, British soldiers, and American soldiers. Even settling into another Christian community would expose them to new attacks. Aside from constantly lurking dangers, the one boy was physically scarred for life, marked, an outcast—he could never go back.

"The terror of the massacre was burned into their memories. In search of peace and solace, they withdrew to a natural refuge not far from here. They became highly skilled in the art of survival and eluding human contact, to the extent that people believed that their hideout was inhabited by phantoms. People would hear voices, see fires burning, but no traces of habitation could be found."

Chills went down my spine. "Do you mean Hermits' Cave?!"

"Exactly," said Dr. Dale knowingly, handing his wife the sugar bowl.

"You can get there through Telanoo! You can see it from Devil's Cranium!"

"We know," Dr. Dale said with a smile.

We sat there in shock.

It suddenly struck me that those fires in Council Cliffs State Park might be the work of two archaeologists digging for our treasure, that maybe the yellowed paper with the phone number was nothing more than a made-up smokescreen to get us off the track!

They suddenly changed the subject and chatted about the tornado damage (which they also knew a lot about), leaving us all rattled from the massacre story and their poking around Magdeline without our knowing.

Aunt Grace came in to chat; high tea lagged on. Finally Aunt Grace got all the compliments she needed, and the Stallards headed for the door with a stack of brochures. The five of us milled around. I was dazed and confused, but mostly ticked off.

Suddenly Dr. Eloise turned to us. "Children!" she said. "There *is* something wrong!" She gave us all piercing looks. "Did the Moravian connection upset you too much? It is history, after all. Those who don't learn from history are doomed to repeat it."

"It's not that," I said.

She shook her head. "Well, something is certainly wrong."

I gave Reece a nudge, hoping she'd take over.

"What?" Reece said. "Me?"

I nodded.

She cleared her throat and faced the Stallards. "Well, um . . . it's about the journals."

"Yes, let us know when you want to discuss them. Our schedules are freer in the summer, "Dr. Eloise said.

Reece braced herself. "We were told that a person stole . . . er . . . took them from the police station. She—the lady at the station—said that the person who took them looked . . . like you, and signed your name."

Dr. Eloise gasped. Her hand flew to her throat. "You think I—"

"We didn't want to think that, but—"

"Well!" she blinked at her husband.

Reece cried, "It's not that we want to think you stole . . . I mean took them. And if you borrowed them, that's okay. We just wondered why you didn't tell us."

Dr. Dale exclaimed, "I don't believe this!"

Rob jumped in. "And then from what Charlie at Florence's said, we were wondering if you were actually—"

I elbowed him in the ribs. "One thing at a time," I said. "Reece is telling it straight. We didn't make this up."

Dr. Dale frowned. "This is most inconvenient and unsettling. An imposter?"

Dr. Eloise said, "I wish you had said something. But no matter." She peeked out the curtain. "We are in an awkward situation." She turned to her husband with one jerk. "Dale. We have a side trip to make. Let us face our accusers and squash this lie!"

We set out for the police station. I should say here that the scientists had loaded us all in their new seven-passenger van, which was perfect for kidnapping. I went on alert in case the van suddenly filled with poison gas or something. I don't know what got into me, but I pictured them whipping out gas masks, at which time I'd reach over the seat and get Dr. Dale in a headlock. Holding my breath, I'd thrust my right leg between the seats, slam on the brakes, throw open the door, and shove him out, saving the day. But nothing like that really happened. We rode along at thirty miles an hour with Rob calmly pointing out the path of the tornado and talking about "updrafts in the vortex." Anyway, when we got to the station, Dr. Eloise's plan hit a snag. The dispatcher—the one who'd let crime evidence slip into the greedy hands of a journal snatcher—was on a two-week vacation in Florida.

Dr. Eloise, aka the dead or missing Mrs. Dowland, drummed her fingers on the counter. "Two weeks. Unacceptable."

"She's been gone a few days already," said the young guy behind the desk. "She'll be back—"

"Not good enough." Dr. Eloise drummed some more, muttering about common criminals dragging her name through the mud.

Looking deep in thought, Skid's green eyes slid to me. "Criminal. Identity."

I nodded. "Mug shot. Sure, why not?" I turned to Dr. Eloise. "We could take your picture and send it to her."

She spun to the guy behind the desk. "You do have an address or phone number where this person can be reached?"

The guy at the counter stammered, "Y-y-yes, but we don't need to—"

She slapped the counter. "We certainly do! It may be irregular, but I will not have these children thinking the worst of me. I will not be suspected of stealing evidence."

She whirled back to Skid and me. "Brilliant, boys! One look at my photo will clear my name." She spun toward the guy again. "Now where do you take the pictures? Shall I come back there?"

The desk guy clearly thought he was dealing with a loon, but the five of us made thin smiles and said it was a good idea.

While we waited for Dr. Eloise to get her mug shot, Dr. Dale asked us in more detail where we were searching for the shoes. I hesitated to give him any clues while the verdict on his wife was still out. I said, "The park is spread out over several sites. We're searching one at a time," which seemed to satisfy him.

Dr. Eloise came out looking happy as a clam. "There! That will be fixed in two shakes of a lamb's tail," she announced. "Now we must be going; we have a lecture to attend in Indianapolis tonight. Let us know when I am vindicated."

I felt I needed to say something. "Thanks for bringing the breastplate back. And thanks for all your work on it. We're sorry to doubt you."

She patted my back. "How could you not? You had the testimony of a credible eyewitness and every right to be skeptical. But in the future, please be forthright. I am all about getting at the truth—you should know that now. Next on the agenda: trace that phone number!"

Chapter 7

※※※

AROUND town there was still a lot of general edginess about the tornado. If only they could have seen that things were actually better than before. The town looked spiffier than it had in ages. Where The Roanoke hotel once stood, a new jewelry store and offices were going in.

Aunt Grace said that insurance companies call a tornado an act of God. A lot of townspeople called ours a disaster, Mother Nature on a rampage. I was confused, but I hardly had time to think about tornadoes or journals or the Moravian connection or even the breastplate of righteousness. I was up to my armpits in Camp Mudj. It was a First-Timers Week—the high-maintenance kids who whine and fall down a lot. Two counselors had poison ivy so bad that Dad had to take them to the emergency room in Columbus. And I wanted to clobber Brad, the ringleader of the counselors, when I caught him sleeping on the picnic table while his team wandered out toward the highway. Bo and Mom and I were picking up the slack.

The whole Bloocifer thing would have died down, except an anonymous counselor kept the fear alive by hanging a "Wanted: Bloocifer, Dead or Alive" poster on the dining room door. A big blue head with fangs dripping blood met all the kids coming for breakfast. Dad had a fit when he saw it.

Rubber snakes appeared in bunks and hanging from rafters. Screams rang out one night when a fake Bloocifer showed up in one of the girls' toilets. The number of campers with terminal homesickness shot way up. I'm all for a joke, but these counselors didn't know when to quit. At the end of the week, Dad shoved a $20 bill in my hand for no reason and said, "You're worth a million of these."

"Thanks, Dad," I said. "Is this enough to buy a couple of railroad ties?"

"Railroad ties?"

"It's just a project. I want to try to make something . . . on my own," I added.

He studied me. "Okay. Don't take anything without asking first."

"Yeah," I agreed, thinking about the journal thief. "Words to live by."

I can't really say what possessed me to build a road through Telanoo. I'd thought about it before and decided it was a dumb idea—all that work for a road to nowhere. But it kept nagging at me, a picture in my mind of the five of us zipping through the wilderness—our private domain—all the way to Devil's Cranium. Reece loved the view from up there. I even wondered if, with Dowland dead and the five of us hanging out back there, Telanoo just might come alive again—like in *The Secret Garden* that Mom was reading to the twins at bedtime. Not that I wanted Telanoo full of roses and blooming trees like Aunt Grace's backyard. But some life would help. Actually it was already greener than it had been in the past few years, but I chalked that up to the wet June.

I'd already decided to start building my road right behind The Cedars, so no one but us (maybe Bo and Dad too) would know it was there. Maneuvering the golf cart off the paved path and around The Cedars to the new road would be no trouble. After that, the shortest route to Devil's Cranium went across a deep, narrow gully, and I needed two railroad ties to start my bridge. It was my deep, dark secret. I was working on it only in the day. Sure, I'd gotten more used to being in Telanoo alone at night, but those illegal fires had people talking about a satanic cult and how there would be vigilante action by the citizens if the police couldn't catch them in the act.

I personally suspected the Brill brothers since they'd been getting into drugs supplied by Mitch Bigelow.

The dispatcher, named Patsy McClain, sent word from Florida that the mug shot of Dr. Eloise was not the face of the journal snatcher. When she got back from vacation, we went in to the station to get the full story. Patsy was about thirty with thick, dark hair. As soon as we identified ourselves as the kids on the Dowland case, she fastened her big, brown eyes on us and started apologizing. "I just wasn't on the ball that day. Who'd think that an old woman would rip off a police station? She walked in, said she was involved with the Dowland case and might have some answers, but that she needed to see the journals. I saw the note about you kids and the scientific data from a Chicago lab with the signature of a Dr. Stallard. She identified herself as such."

"She said her name was Eloise Stallard?" Reece asked in disbelief.

"There's where I made the mistake and again I'm sorry, though I don't believe the case has been compromised," she said defensively. "It's all but officially closed. I was reading over the information as I brought out the case file. I put it there on the counter, and I took a call over at my desk. I came back, glanced at the report, and said, 'It looks like we can release these only to some teens or to this Dr. Stallard.' The woman gave me a strange look and said, 'Yes. That's right.' I asked, 'Oh, are you Dr. Eloise Stallard?' She stammered and then said yes. She didn't actually say she was Dr. Stallard until I mentioned the name. I took another call—we were shorthanded that day—and when I came back, she was gone."

"What did she look like?" Rob asked.

"Small, older lady. Short, curled hair, brownish-grayish. Rimless glasses. Pushing seventy. Quite a nervous, jittery type."

"But that's her!" Rob cried.

The dispatcher shook her head. "Similar but not the same as the mug shot. The woman who took the journals had a round face, larger eyes, a little more gray in the hair."

Mei said, "Dr. Eloise has a thin face and small eyes."

Reece said, "Hey, I know! If you could describe her, Mei could draw her. She's an artist."

"Is that so?" asked Patsy.

Mei covered her face with both hands. I couldn't tell if she was embarrassed or scared. "Nooo," she moaned, "I caaaan't."

Mei tried to back out, but we wouldn't let her. "Give it a try, please, Mei," Reece said.

One thing led to another. Patsy brought out a pad and pencil, described the lady, and before long Mei had done a simple sketch.

Patsy said, "That's pretty close. Yes, that's her. Add a few more wrinkles around her eyes and make the chin a little fuller. Good. This is definitely not the same person as the mug shot." She huffed. "I was bamboozled. That old woman seemed so fragile and nervous about being in a police station. But she was snookering me the whole time!"

Skid asked, "Can we take this sketch or make a copy of it?"

Patsy wanted to know why.

"You're shorthanded, right? We want to help. I'll ask the Romeos; they know everything."

It was just after lunchtime, the crowd was thin, the Romeos gone. The five of us scooted into a booth at Florence's. We ordered fries and drinks.

"What are we here for?" Reece asked.

Skid leaned in and raised an eyebrow. "Looking for informants."

We didn't have to wait long. Two ladies came in—one regular size and wearing a print dress, the other one chunky with pinkish blond hair and a purple sweat suit. They sat down and got coffee.

Skid nodded. "Jackpot. They'll be better than the Romeos." He handed the sketch to me. Charm their socks off, Creek."

"You go," I said. "You know how to do this."

"I scare people. Go on."

I slid out of the booth and approached them. "Excuse me," I said.

They looked up at me like I was planning to mug them. I got down on one knee between them, following the law of the wild, which says to assume a stance of submission when you confront a foe and don't want to fight. I heard Rob snort behind me. I said, "Um, I have this picture of a person, and I need to find her, but I don't know if she's from Magdeline or not. Do you know if she lives around here?"

I laid the picture down. They puzzled over it.

The pink-haired lady said, "She doesn't look familiar to me, but I've not lived here my whole life. Do you know who that is, Helen?"

"Can't say I do. Something familiar about her, though." After a minute she shook her head. "The Poe girls would know. They taught school here for forty years. They might be able to tell you."

"The Poe girls?" I repeated.

"Ruby and Rose. They live on Charlotte Heights. House number 111. It's the yellow two-story with the red geraniums hanging on the porch."

I got up and tipped my head at them. "Thank you."

"They'll be home," said the pink-haired one. "They never go anywhere. Miss Ruby taught my children and my grandchildren. She was a disciplinarian back in the days when that was allowed."

"I'll ask them."

"Tell them Lydia Percival sent you."

I backed away. "Okay."

"Such a nice young man, isn't he?" Helen said to Lydia as if I weren't there.

"Yes, he is," Lydia said. "What's your name, son?"

I kept backing. "Elijah Creek."

"From the camp?"

"Yes, ma'am."

"Polite, isn't he?" Lydia said. "So many children today are terribly rude. It's shameful! He's such a nice boy. I've met his mother; she does clothing drives."

I slid back into the booth.

Rob snickered, "You looked like you were proposing."

"Shut up, will you; I got a good lead: 111 Charlotte Heights. Some old schoolteachers who know everybody."

Skid said, "You go, Elijah. We'll wait here and polish off the fries."

"Your turn," I said.

"I'm telling you, I scare people. They'd never open the door."

Rob and I took off jogging down Main, me wondering if Skid always wore black as a rebel statement against prejudice: *if you think I'm a threat, then maybe I am, so back off.*

Four blocks later we cut right at Charlotte Heights. We slowed to a walk when we reached the wrought iron gate of house number 111. It was a tiny yard full of shrubs and flowers and lawn ornaments. Red geraniums hung from the porch ceiling. We knocked on the door. A few minutes passed.

"Should we knock again?" Rob whispered.

Something moved behind the lace-covered door pane. "Wait," I said.

A crackly voice from inside said, "We don't want cookies or magazines."

"We're not selling." I held the sketch up to the door. "We're looking for someone, and your friend Lydia Percival said you might know her."

Two faces moved behind the curtain. I heard murmurings; the door creaked open. They were the tallest, skinniest old women you could imagine. They had steel-gray hair, pointy chins, little round, rimless glasses, and dark dresses with white collars. The Poe girls hadn't been "girls" for a century.

"Lydia?" one asked.

"She said you might know this person."

They looked at the sketch through the screen door.

"Well, I can't be sure. It's been many years, and my memory's not what it used to be."

"It's Francine, isn't it?" said the other sister.

"I believe it is."

"It's her, but older."

They looked at us, confused. "We think it's Francine Dowland, but she passed away some years ago."

For the third time that summer, you could have knocked me over with a feather. Rob asked, "Would that be . . . Stan Dowland's wife?"

"That's right. Didn't he just pass away over in Newpoint?"

"It's been a few months," Rob said.

She shook her head sadly. "Such a sad man. May he rest in peace. That can't be Francine, boys. She passed away. Maybe she had a sister."

Rob and I tore back into Florence's with a racket; everyone turned and stared. As we slid into the booth, I let Rob do the talking.

"You'll never, ever guess. Not in a million years!"

Skid said, "Dowland's wife."

I huffed at him for stealing my thunder.

The girls gasped. Reece's jaw dropped, "Then it's true!"

"And everyone in town thinks she's dead!" Rob yelled.

The people in Florence's turned and stared.

Skid leaned in to us. "And everyone based that idea on Dowland's stories: his daughter moved, his wife died. The Romeos only knew what Dowland told them."

Rob sat back in a stupor. Reece stared at me in shock.

"Sugoi, sugoi!" Mei breathed, her almond-shaped eyes wide and scared.

It was like a huge light came on for all of us.

Skid thought out loud. "She left him. Seriously embarrassing for a preacher. Better for a guy to say his wife died than that she dumped him and never came back."

"Where has she been all this time?" Rob asked. "Not married to Dr. Dale, anyway!"

"My question is, where is she now and what is she up to?" I asked sharply.

"Call the police," Reece said.

Mei moaned, "More trouble?"

Skid jostled her in a friendly way. "We're cool, Mei, we're cool."

I didn't say anything, but I suddenly wondered if with Francine Dowland back from the dead, we'd just lost our exclusive claim to the armor of God.

Chapter 8

MY mom dropped us off at our next exploration site in Council Cliffs State Park with the usual, "Stay together now."

"Earshot," I said back and headed across the parking lot. "We'll stay in earshot."

"Eyeshot, Elijah."

"Okay."

"Promise?"

"Promise."

"And Mei's mom is picking you up?"

"Yes. She has a driver's license now."

"Before dark?"

"Right."

"It gets dark in the gorge first."

"I know, Mom." Heading down into the gorge, I raised the back of my fist and pointed to it, my signal that I knew the place like the back of my hand.

"Hermits' Cave is the coolest of the gorges," I told the others as we set out that afternoon. "It has the second biggest overhanging ledge, a deep stream with blue-green water, and a swirling pool called the Vortex. There are tunnels and bridges and side trails. The main trail connects up to Eagle Rock Falls, so I can show you that at the other end. And you know what? It's the closest to the ruin where we found Dowland's daughter. Remember how the broken compass pointed to the ruin? Well, Hermits' Cave is in a straight line beyond that, east-northeast from Devil's Cranium. You can even see part of the rim from there. If Dowland buried the shoes anywhere in the park, I have a feeling they'll be here. All of these gorges were hideouts for Indian war councils."

At the trail head I said, "Reece and Mei, you follow the main path to the stone bridge at the far end of the gorge, but not over the rise to Eagle Rock Falls. We'll all go there together. Rob, you take as many side trails in the gorge as you can; Skid, you take the west rim trail. I'll do the east rim. It works out about the same lengthwise. And everyone check the slopes around your trails. Look for a fresh dig and meet up at the bridge. There are lots of steps there. Reece, you okay?"

"Yeah, just a little tired. It's hot."

Rob said, "It's supposed to rain later, so we don't have long."

I took off for the upper trail and shot back, "It's just water! We have until dark!"

Rob zigzagged; Skid and I circled the gorge. I stayed in earshot of everyone and had at least one in view almost all the time. There were other hikers in the park. I kept track of them too and paid extra close attention to the landmarks: sharp turns, roots, broken branches on the trail. I took a break to examine the wooden bridges spanning the gullies to see how they were put together. My bridge in Telanoo wouldn't be as good as one built by engineers, but it would have one advantage: it would be almost invisible.

I ran from the rim up the slope, covered ground looking for anything like a freshly dug spot, then ran back to check on everyone's locations. Every now and then I spotted Skid through the trees across the canyon, moving in the same direction at the same speed. Sometimes he seemed not like a person, but my shadow who'd cut himself free but stayed close. He almost matched my steps, moving up the hill into the deep woods away from the gorge, then running back down to the edge of the rim to report in. "Anything?" he'd call across the chasm.

"Nothing," I'd call back.

"Nothing down here," Rob or Reece would call up to us from the bottom of the gorge.

Again and again, "Anything?" I'd ask.

"Nothing," they'd answer.

"I'm going to need those shoes of peace when I find them," I said to God. "'Cause I'm wearing mine out fast."

Knowing that Francine Dowland was alive and in possession of the journals, I worried that she had a search party out for our treasure. *Was it really ours?* I wondered as I covered ground. *If her husband bought it but buried it and then died, if she was married to him at the time he bought it, was it hers? What about the pieces we already had?* Once again, I needed a lawyer.

The rim trails ended at the first falls. Skid and I stood on opposite sides of the stream, just a few yards apart but unable to cross. Water roared over the slippery seventy-foot drop. I gave him a questioning look in case he'd found something. He shook his head. Nothing.

We edged toward the cliff and yelled down at Reece and Rob and Mei.

They waved up at us, squinting in the sun, and yelled something, but we couldn't hear for the falls.

I sat on a nearby log to catch my breath. The story of the two Delaware boys came back to me, just as the Stallards had told it. . . .

My problems—a snake on the loose and a pack of lazy counselors—were small potatoes compared to losing everyone and living life alone. Sure I liked my aloneness, craved it sometimes. But only because I had friends and family waiting back home.

What if there wasn't even a house to go back to? The heat of summer, the dead of winter . . .

The story of the Delaware boys laid heavy on my mind. What would it be like to have no one?

I glanced across the stream at Skid. He was looking down toward Reece, Rob, and Mei in the gorge but with a faraway, thoughtful expression. He was thinking about the Moravian connection too. I caught his eye and held up two fingers. *Are you thinking about the two boys who lived here?* I was asking.

He grinned at me for a minute, then made a cross with his index fingers. Next he drew one finger sharply across his wrist and rubbed his wrists together. He raised two fingers like I had, but this time he meant peace. I nodded that I understood.

Two boys. Christians. Blood brothers. Peace.

He hiked back to the opposite side of the gorge and worked his way down a rugged path to the bottom. He talked to the others a few minutes, all of them standing down there in a patch of sunlight. I was deaf to them because of the waterfall, but something in the way they looked around without saying a word told me they were thinking about the hermit boys. Sure, we'd read about religious persecution and the struggle for freedom in history class, but it hadn't hit home until now—at least not with me. I was standing where they had stood, walking their path, hearing their waterfall, breathing their air.

I backtracked from the falls, went to the lip of the big ledge overhanging Hermits' Cave, and held onto a tree. "How's it going down there?"

Mei gasped. "You're standing on nothing!"

I laughed. "It'll hold. Been here for centuries."

Rob slapped a boulder as big as the Stallards' new van. "Oh yeah? About ten years ago, this was up there."

I held my ground, but my knees got a little weak.

Rob said, "We're finding hundreds of stash holes in these cliffs. Thousands."

Skid said, "People are stashing stuff all over the place."

"Anybody could have taken the shoes of peace!" Reece cried.

I leaned over the edge and spoke low, "Shhhh! You're not alone." I pointed down to their left. They listened. Two couples in hiking gear were heading in their direction. I saw them, and in a few seconds the others heard them. "Wait there," I called.

I found a fissure in the cliff wall, a steep, dripping crevice. Not exactly a trail, but it was passable.

"This is impossible," Rob said when I reached the bottom. "Mei found a full beer bottle in one hole and a book in a plastic bag in another."

Reece sighed pitifully. "I found a piece of wood that said *Hello Ty from Andrea*. We found clothes too, a pair of jeans and an old hat; people leave stuff all over the place for each other."

Her face was red, and she was breathing hard. She'd never sounded so discouraged.

"He buried them here. I'm sure of it," I insisted. "Because of the raven."

Rob emptied his canteen and wiped his face. "See the sandy places under the ledges? There are a dozen sites like that. The shoes could be buried anywhere in those acres of sand."

"We'll bring in the metal detector. Anyway, Dowland would have left a marker so he could find the spot again."

"Not if he made a map," Rob argued.

They all looked hot and tired. "Take a break," I said. I led them to a shady outcropping of rock that overhung the creek. We drank water, ate our sandwiches, and dangled our feet in the stream. Mei offered each of us a hankie. Reece blotted her face. We guys doused our hankies in water and tied them around our necks.

"We push on," I said. "But only go as far up each hill as an old man would," I told them. "We got a late start today, so we may not get done before dark. Remember, it gets dark in the gorge sooner than up on the rim."

Reece patted her face and took another drink. Breathlessly she said, "No sign of the raven, I guess."

"No sign," I said.

Skid and Rob headed off through the tunnel for one more sweep of the side trails. I scouted out the rim trail toward Eagle Rock Falls, but had pretty much decided that Dowland wouldn't have buried the shoes along the rim. The area was too rugged, and parts of the rim trail often washed out and had to be rerouted. Big hunks of the ledge were broken and lying in heaps on the canyon floor. Besides that, an untrained eye would have a tough time finding landmarks anyway; trees and rocks and cliffs look alike to people who don't know nature.

I didn't want to give up. After another half hour, when I hadn't heard any whoops of discovery, I made my way back to the overlook above the bridge to see if the others were done. Reece was leaning over the bridge like she was throwing up.

"Hey!" I called down.

Mei ran to the foot of the cliff and looked straight up at me. "She can't walk more, Elijah. Too much. All of a sudden she has terrible pain. *Taihen!*"

By the time I got down to the bridge, Reece was on the ground, propped against the stone bridge, white as a sheet and shivering.

I tried to sound calm. "What's going on?"

"We're almost done," Reece said. "Mei can finish . . . and I'll rest . . . here."

Mei leaned into my sight line and shook her head, telling me that she wasn't going another step.

"We've done enough for one day," I said. "It's getting dark."

Reece's breathing was shallow, sweat popping out on her forehead. A stab of fear went through me. *Shock,* I thought. I'd seen the symptoms once before when a kid at camp broke his arm so bad the bone came through the skin and he made the big mistake of looking at it.

"Did you hurt yourself?"

"It just started," she gasped.

"Don't move," I ordered. "Mei, get our gear together. Where are the guys?"

"I don't know!" she cried. "That way and that way?"

I yelled their names in all directions until I heard whoops.

They probably thought we'd found the treasure and would be disappointed, but too bad. I needed them fast. I met them in the tunnel and lost the calm tone I'd used on Reece. "We've got trouble. Reece can't make it back out by herself."

"Are you serious?" Skid asked.

Rob's eyes got big. "What happened?"

"I don't know. Follow me." By the time we were within sight of the girls, Reece was on the ground, her head in Mei's lap. I stopped the guys and whispered, "It looks like shock: shallow breathing, pale, sweat, and chills."

"Shock?" Rob asked. "What's that mean?"

"It means something's happening, and her body's shutting down to fix it. It can be serious if we wait too long."

Skid's green eyes glowed at me in the fading light. "What are you talking about?"

"I mean we get help now!"

Reece tried to stand; but when that didn't work, we tried making a saddle with our arms to carry her up the trail. She cried out in agony after a few feet.

"Stop!" I yelled. "We're putting her down." We sat her down gently, and she fell back on the ground crying and clutching her leg. I knelt. "Okay, Reece, here's the deal. We keep your head lower than your body so you don't pass out."

Mei sat beside her and stroked her forehead. "What can I do? Rest in my lap again. I'll stay with you."

"Wait! I said we have to keep her head *lower* than her body! *Lower!* You get out to the road as fast as you can," I told her. "Your Mom should be there by now."

"Which way?" she looked confused.

"That way. Eagle Rock Falls entrance. Just stay on the main path."

"Entrance?"

"Yeah, the road on the other side where we're heading. You know, we started at one end of the canyon and we're ending at the other—at Eagle Rock Falls."

Her eyes got big. "Other end? There's a road at the other end?"

I gaped at her. "Yeah. Didn't you tell your mom to meet us there?"

"I told my mother to meet us at the same place! I thought—"

"But that's more than a mile back that way!" I yelled.

"I showed you the map, Mei!" Rob snapped. "I showed you the end!"

"I didn't understand!" she said.

"But I showed you how the main canyon ran from one road to another!"

"I'm sorry!" her eyes squeezed shut, big tears ran down her face. "I thought we go to the end and come back!"

"Stop!" Reece said weakly. "It doesn't hurt that bad if I don't move, so I'll rest here. No rush, okay? *Daijoubu,* Mei. Really, *daijoubu.* Piece of cake."

"Sorry, Mei," I said. "We didn't mean to yell. We'll figure it out. Don't cry." I turned to Skid. "You go try to flag someone down."

He laughed coldly. "Are you kidding? A black kid on a back road at sundown. No one will stop for me."

I ran my hand through my hair. *Okay, think!* "Okay, Rob, you go. Flag someone down and tell them to call an ambulance."

"An ambulance?!"

"Go!" I ordered. "Mei, you go to the other road and tell your mom to call an ambulance. No, wait. Tell her to call Reece's mom. No, *you* call Reece's mom. Your mom doesn't understand English. And we don't want two ambulances."

Rob said, "Reece's mom will call an ambulance—"

"Okay, it doesn't matter," I barked at Mei in frustration. "Just go!"

Rob said worriedly, "Wait a minute . . . Mei, do you know the way back? Elijah, shouldn't you go? You're the fastest."

"Mei's mom won't understand my English. She'll panic," I answered, looking at Reece lying there still as death. "I'm not leaving," I said.

"I know the way! I can go!" Mei insisted.

"Yeah, but it's getting dark," I worried out loud, rethinking my plan. "You shouldn't be by yourself. Not with strange fires burning at night—"

"I'll run fast," she insisted. "No one will catch me!"

I thought Skid should go with her until I glanced at the

sky. The sun had crept down behind the cliff, and a damp chill was already settling in the hollow. If there was a gang of satanists lurking around, I wasn't about to leave Reece with only me to guard her. I'm brave, but I'm no idiot.

"Let Mei go," came Reece's little voice from the ground. "She can do it."

"Okay, we stay here," I said solidly to Skid.

Rob took off toward Eagle Rock Falls. Mei pulled the crystal out of her pocket, whispered something to herself, and took off in the opposite direction.

"Run!" I called after her. "And don't forget your way back. Pay attention! We're at the bridge below the cave!"

I turned back to Skid and whispered, "We have to keep her calm."

He leaned in nose-to-nose. "Then you need to put on your game face, Creek. You're freakin' on us."

I gulped in air, heaved it out, and went down on one knee. "Okay, Reece, what's going on?"

Reece shook her head. "I don't know . . . it hurts so bad!"

I calculated that Rob wouldn't reach the back road for fifteen minutes even at full tilt, and who knew when a car would come by, or even if they would stop. I imagined Rob by himself on that road in the dark and thought about those mysterious fire-starters sneaking their way into the park after hours, probably by the back way. A chill went through me. *Be careful, cousin. Don't catch a ride with just anybody.*

If she ran full speed, Mei would reach the road in maybe

twenty minutes. It could be another half hour before an ambulance came, an hour to bring a stretcher back in. None of us had brought jackets. We had no blankets, and over the damp, woodsy smells of the gorge, I could smell rain coming in with the dark.

Every minute or so Reece shivered hard and groaned in pain. Her face against the dark ground shone white in the twilight gloom. Her forehead and cheeks looked as thin and fragile as Aunt Grace's china. We were a good thirty yards from being under the cliff shelf where it was sandy and warm. "Reece," I said calmly, "it's going to rain. We have to move you."

She didn't want to. "So what? It's just water. Isn't that what you always say, Elijah, 'it's just water'?"

"The sand is soft up there. It would be more comfortable than this hard, packed dirt. The ground is sapping the heat from you."

"I can't move."

"But you're shivering, and we have a while to wait." I turned to Skid. "Okay, then. You get sand, I'll get fire."

Skid used his T-shirt as a bag and brought down sand to put under Reece. He made jokes about being at the beach. He and I told her stuff about our adventures at Farr Island. When he tied the last load into a pillow, I gathered leaves and twigs and assembled a little fire beside her.

"That's illegal," she said as she watched me.

"So they can throw me in the slammer," I said with a

grin. "I'm supposed to stand by while your teeth rattle out of your head?" Lying on cold, hard ground is the worst thing if you're in shock, so I started another fire close to her other side and watched every stray spark.

The narrow strip of sky between the upper edges of the canyon had turned blue-gray—the temperature was dropping. "An evening storm is coming. We have maybe a half an hour. It could pass us by, but I doubt it."

Skid went up under the ledge so he could watch for Rob or Mei. Reece lay quiet except for a sudden fit of shivers now and then. Between shivers she gazed up at the sky with this great little smile on her face.

"What?" I asked.

"The clouds are so pretty. The way they move so fast above . . . it looks like the trees are moving, like everything's floating, like we're drifting along and the sky is standing still."

I sat down beside her and leaned against the stone bridge. I looked up too. "Yeah. Every time I come here, I think it would be the best place to live."

"It would. I love the sound of the water and the smell of the air." She was quiet for a long time. "Thanks for having Skid bring the sand down."

"I'll tell him to bring more."

"That's okay." She was breathing more calmly. "Hey . . . how hard would it be to live out here?"

I added twigs to the fires. "Fire would be easy with all the dead trees and leaves. You have good shelter in the caves. They're not deep, but you'd be surprised how warm a good overhang can be. Build a couple of stone walls and a roof of forest debris. Good shelter."

"God gave us everything we needed, didn't he?"

"Yeah, and there's plenty of clean water with the falls. Hey, are you thirsty? The canteen's empty, but see the drips coming out of that cliff? That's a vein of water. It's pretty pure from seeping through the rocks." I collected a few inches in the water bottle. She drank it all.

I took it back and sat it under the drips. "We'll have more in a few minutes." I sat back down and fed the fires. "Food would be the biggest problem with living out here. The creeks are too shallow to have much in the way of fish—a few crayfish maybe. You see squirrel and quail but not much. There are deer out here, but you'd have to know how to dress and preserve them. You could survive a while off roots and berries. I don't know a whole lot about that yet. I'm sure the hermits knew a lot of secrets of survival that even I don't know."

We sat there by the stream and listened to the soft crackles of the little fires. In the cool quiet, I almost forgot we were in crisis—Reece and I talking quietly as if we were all alone, Skid up at the cave playing sentry, his eye ranging north, then south for signs of life.

"What about the dangers?" she asked.

"Other than freezing and starving to death, not much.

There are a few kinds of poisonous snakes—massasauga, rattlers, and copperheads—there are coyotes and bobcats, and I've heard that black bears are making a comeback, but I've never seen one around here. Most times wild animals will leave you alone unless they're provoked. You have to know what you're doing."

She said, "Those two boys lived out here for years all by themselves."

"Yeah, but they were Indians."

"You're as good as them. You could do it."

I grinned while my insides did a huge somersault. "Yeah. I guess I could sell firewood and buy food with it. Or train a coyote to steal chickens. I've seen a few wild turkeys come up behind Morgan's farm. I could get one with my bow and arrow."

"Make turkey jerky," she joked.

I fed the fires and kept my eye on Skid as he stood watch up there, shirtless and looking more like his dad every day. I was thinking he'd bulked up since Farr Island. Then it struck me, what I bet he'd been doing on his time off: pumping iron. Marcus Skidmore was right about scaring people. I personally wouldn't want to get on his bad side and run across those mean green eyes glowering at me in a dark alley.

My ears were tuned for Rob and Mei's return or for any sound that wasn't natural. Would my fires draw them—the unknowns out there, the druggies or satanists, or Francine

Dowland's treasure hunters? I wished I knew who we were dealing with.

Reece got really still. Her eyes closed.

My heart thumped. "Reece?"

She smiled. "Just resting. The pillow's nice, and I'm getting warm. The sound of the water and the fire is so peaceful. . . ."

"Yeah."

"I hate to tell you this, Elijah, but you probably already know it: we're not going to find the shoes of peace this way." Her eyes opened and locked onto mine. "Are we?"

I sighed. "Not without a sign."

"I'll pray."

"Okay."

Skid had come down to check on us. "No sign of them yet, Creek. Need any more wood?"

"Not yet."

Reece said, "Guys, pray with me, okay?"

Skid said, "Sure. Since we're stuck here, let's make it an hour of power." He sat cross-legged next to her.

She reached for his hand. "You want to go first?"

"You go."

This praying and holding hands deal was obviously something they did a lot. I felt sort of like a third wheel, not wanting to hold hands with her while Skid was there and feeling weird about taking his hand. I hoped she wouldn't ask me to pray. So far, it had been a private thing between

God and me. I sat there with my arms resting on my knees, my hands knotted in front of me. I half bowed.

Her eyes closed and then came right open again. "Dear God, I just can't keep my eyes closed for this one. What you've made is so awesome. I guess if I was going to hurt myself and be stuck somewhere, this is the best place, so thank you for that. Thank you for Skid's sand pillow and Elijah's fires. Thank you for the cliffs and ferns, the water that's so clear and really blue in the deep places like the Vortex . . . the birds flying overhead and how today the sunlight came through the leaves and made them neon green, the smell of pine trees . . . I love you, God." She sniffled. "Skid, you take over."

He closed his eyes and nodded. His voice was thick. "Yeah, Lord, this is a super place. How you do all this is seriously amazing. Right now we need a couple of things. An ambulance would be nice for starters, or just take Reece's pain so she could walk out of here. But you're the boss. So just do your thing."

"The shoes," Reece reminded.

"Oh yeah. Well, thanks for the raven of general direction, but if we could have something a little more specific, it would save us a lot of time in finding the shoes of peace. You could just tell Elijah; that'd be cool by me."

I watched them like a hawk. Something deep down in me welled up like a geyser. I was thinking, *I want that! I want it!* when big drops started falling. One of my fires sputtered. *Oh, great! Thanks a lot, God!*

Skid said amen, and I jumped to my feet. "Okay, Reece, we have to get you up and into Hermits' Cave. Can you walk, or should we carry you?"

"I can't walk at all. I can't."

Skid went around to her head, reached under her arms, and started to lift. I was ready to scoop my arms under her knees. He lifted, she sucked in a scream, and words came rushing. "Stop! Put me down! Stop!"

"Hey!!" a deep voice bellowed behind us. "What are you boys doing?!"

My heart shot into my throat. I whirled. A man came pounding down the path, pulling out a nightstick as he ran toward us. He was wearing a park uniform. "Step away from her! Leave her alone!!" Suddenly my mind flashed on how this must look: two guys and a screaming girl in the park after hours with fires burning: bad . . . way, way bad.

"Wait! It's okay!" Reece cried weakly. Her head dropped back. "They're—"

"She's hurt!" I said. "We need an ambulance! My dad is—"

"Put her down!!" The ranger looked down at Reece, her face a whitish green by now. He glared at us. "What do you creeps think you're doing?!"

Chapter 9

ONCE we'd explained ourselves—Reece backing up every word we said—the park ranger radioed for help. Somehow everyone but Rob congregated at the back entrance of the park about the same time. Mom asked me a ton of questions, and Reece's mom filled in the emergency medical people about Reece's condition. They didn't let anyone but her mom ride in the ambulance. Mrs. Elliston asked my mom to please see that her car got back to town and to please call Reece's dad and tell him the news.

My last glimpse of Reece was her biting her lip in pain as they loaded her into the back of the ambulance—red lights flashing onto her face. Mei struggled to hold Reece's hand while her mom was talking to her a mile a minute in Japanese. Skid stood there like a bodyguard, his sandy T-shirt slung over his shoulder.

What happened and whose fault was it? they all asked. Naturally everyone was looking to me for answers. Feeling responsible for my clan, I answered the best I could and kept asking about Rob, insisting that the medical team radio the police and get a network going to track him down. I mentioned Officer Taylor and Patsy McClain by name. I tried not to panic.

After the ambulance left, Mom got us together by the

roadside with Mei and her mom and explained things while Mei interpreted. News came through the park ranger's radio that Rob had been picked up and was home safe, but I wanted confirmation. When we dropped off Skid at his condo, Mom and I ran in to call Aunt Grace. Sure enough, Rob had gotten a ride on the back of a motorcycle from a guy who worked at the service station. I filled Rob in on the rest while Mom was telling Carlotta.

When we got home, Mom grilled me—not accusing exactly, but it was in her tone. Had Reece been walking the gorge that whole time? Had she complained before the incident? Did her mother know she'd be walking all day?

Sitting at the kitchen table, drowning my troubles in a plate of leftovers, I wondered myself if I'd pushed too hard. I couldn't blame the moms; I'd have been firing questions at people too if I'd seen Reece coming out of a canyon on a stretcher, white and shivering and crying.

"I don't know what happened, Mom. She suddenly got worse and kind of went down. So I did what I thought was best."

When Dad got in later, we went through it all again.

"She just went down," was all I could say. "She just went down."

"You did the right thing, Elijah," Dad said finally. "You sent for help and tried to make her comfortable. Even building the fire, under the circumstances, was the right idea. I'm sure the park authorities will understand."

I wouldn't have slept worse on a bed of nails. All night long I tossed. It stormed—usually the best sleeping weather—but every raindrop splattering the window rattled my head. In the wee hours, I even stood in the middle of my room to wear myself out, half hoping I'd fall asleep, crack a bone, and end up in the hospital myself. I didn't remember going back to sleep until I woke up across the bed—my eyes like sandpaper—wondering what they'd done to Reece.

Was it my fault? I asked myself, sitting there in the dark of my room. *Had Reece ignored warning signs because she was following my orders?* I sat on my bed, propped against the wall with the lights out. I stared into the darkness. *How were we supposed to keep the armor of God a secret when we kept making headlines?*

Prepare to find peace, came Dr. Eloise's voice.

Yeah, right.

The next morning I stumbled downstairs where Mom was folding laundry on the kitchen table. It was almost 10:00. I hoped the counselors were up to snuff so I wouldn't be needed today.

"What about Reece?" I asked.

"She's in surgery this morning. I'm sure she'll be fine, Elijah." She gave me a cheesy grin. "You like her, don't you?"

"Surgery? Why?" My eyes closed again, but my backside managed to find the kitchen chair.

"Apparently there are problems with the joint again, some kind of splinters growing on it. I don't understand how that can happen, but . . ." Mom shuddered. "It must be excruciating, the poor little thing. The doctors are amazed at her resilience."

"Will she be able to walk?"

"Oh, I couldn't ask her mother that, honey!"

"Can we go?"

"To Columbus?" Mom stacked towels. "She'll be groggy most of the day. Her mom will decide when she can have visitors. Not to change the subject, but we're starting to get those baskets of vegetables from the neighbors like we do every summer. I'll need you to sort through them. Take the best down to the dining hall, bring the castoffs here. I'll make soup."

"If Skid and his mom go to the hospital, can I ride along?"

"Check with your dad in case he needs you. It's still wet out, which means—you know what that means—we're on call for camp duty." She made a sound of frustration. "I can't believe these college kids. They get more lax every year. Nori and Stacy have better leadership skills. It's ridiculous!" She grabbed up a towel from the pile, took it by the corners, and gave it an angry snap. I made myself toast while she ranted on and folded towels. "The college program is supposed to be an internship—for credit—and they act like it's one big vacation!" She snapped another towel. "Somewhere there's a serious gap in the educational system."

I said, "They need to be dropped off in Telanoo for a month with nothing but a pocket knife."

She grinned wickedly at me. "There you go."

"I'm never going to college," I said.

"Oh, yes you are! You can't get a decent job without a college education. We have to start thinking about that now." She stacked towels in the laundry basket and headed upstairs. "Have some hot chocolate. It's cool out."

I took a mug out on the porch and sat on the rail. Camp Mudjokivi spread out cool and gray-green in front of me— the lake water rippled and white, the dark blue shadows of Owl Woods as still as a picture. The campus was empty except for a few stragglers who were late for their classes. The morning drizzle had stopped, but the sky was heavy. My thoughts drifted back to late winter when the five of us were drinking Aunt Grace's gourmet hot chocolate at The Castle and the raven came. Even then Reece was shivering with the cold, struggling to walk, but urging us on to search for the armor of God. She told Rob to have faith and reminded us of everything we'd accomplished in one semester. I couldn't ignore the nagging feeling that I'd pushed her too hard.

I was still pretty new at praying, so I just said in my head, *When you're looking in on Reece, God, don't forget that shoes of peace are for walking. You're the boss, so your will be done. Amen. PS. Shoes. Walking. Reece. You know what I'm getting at?*

There'd be no outdoor sports today, no swimming. The grass was deep and too wet for the mowers to come—perfect for Bloocifer. I hadn't forgotten about him and wondered if he'd forgotten about me. I was the one who'd caught him in the first place, and every time I'd press my face to the glass or drop a frozen mouse into his cage, he always had a special threat for me: a lunge at the glass like he wanted to sink his fangs into me. Or he'd wiggle his forked tongue, picking up my scent before he slithered under his rock. I began to think of all the places he might be hiding: around the pool under the flowerpots of the cabana, in the rafters of the gazebo by the lake, in the swamp near the meadow, hidden under my bed and ready to strike. The snake book said racers are vicious attackers. I knew it firsthand. Funny how a quarter-inch-thick piece of glass can give you so much confidence.

I slugged down the last of the hot chocolate and shook Bloocifer from my mind. If Skid could talk his mom into a trip to Columbus tomorrow, I could use today to make headway on my road through Telanoo. Even if the rain kept up, I could pick up supplies. Bo had—without asking too many questions   helped me haul out the railroad ties I'd bought. I had almost enough wood for the floor of the bridge; it had to be wide enough for the golf cart to get across. There were plenty of nails in the maintenance building. We had hammers and saws. I'd need to make a rail—rope would be cheap. Maybe I'd wind grapevines through the rope to camouflage it. If I cut the boards unevenly and stained them in a camouflage pattern like the ground, the bridge would look like part of Telanoo: the Shadow Bridge, that's what I'd call it. Reece would be so surprised.

A police cruiser pulled slowly into camp. It was Officer Taylor. He turned into the drive, and my heart jumped into my throat. The picture of Reece in the ambulance was still raw in my mind, and with a shudder I thought about how police always come and tell people when their relatives have been killed. The cruiser door opened. I went to the edge of the porch, fixing my gaze on his expression for a clue to his purpose. I couldn't read him. Cops always look the same, good news or bad. He came to the bottom of the steps.

"Morning, Elijah. Just get up?"

"Yeah." I couldn't ask him what was wrong. I just couldn't. I fixed on his face, which told me nothing.

He looked up at me. "Well, son, I'm sorry to have to come—"

My mind fogged, all functions stopped. Oh no . . . *No!* I fell back a step. *NO!*

Chapter 10

"IT'S okay, son," said Officer Taylor, standing at the foot of the porch steps. "I didn't come here to arrest you."

That was no comfort, no comfort at all. "Is it? . . . It's not . . ."

He went on officially, "I'm letting you know about a complaint registered by the parks department about those fires you set last night."

I wasn't listening all the way, but I did start breathing again.

"They understand the situation, Elijah, but the recent occurrences in the park make it necessary to—are you all right, son? You need to sit down? You're not in trouble."

I leaned back against the porch post, still dazed. He was here about the fires . . . not about Reece.

He stood there with one foot on a step, leaning toward me, his arm starting up to catch me. I hadn't read his face, but he read mine. He relaxed and sort of smiled. "It's all good news, Elijah. Reece is out of surgery. She came through okay. I'm here because the park authorities have written up a complaint; it's a formality because of the recent unexplained fires—"

Mom had come to the door just in time to see my stricken face and hear about park authorities complaining.

She gasped, and Officer Taylor had to give the whole spiel over again so she wouldn't blow a gasket.

Then the phone rang and Mom was back in the house. I expected Officer Taylor to leave, but he came up a couple more steps until we were pretty much face-to-face.

He began with, "For the record . . ."

"Okay . . ."

"What were you doing in the park, the five of you?"

Omen, I said to myself. *The truth.* "Looking for a piece of that old armor."

"Do you have any information regarding the other fires?"

"No, sir."

He kept looking at me like he wanted more. I said, "I'd never do anything stupid like leave a fire burning in a park. I know how to make one with hardly any smoke and leave no trace when I'm done. That's the responsible way."

He paused. "What about that fire you built at the old Theobald place last fall? I found that one."

"It was in a pile of junk. I wasn't trying to hide anything, and I put it out before we left it. Good and out."

He nodded. "Smart kid." He headed back toward his car and turned. "You know that park well, don't you?"

I lifted my fist and pointed to it. "Like the back of my hand."

Officer Taylor grinned at me. "You're a good resource."

He got in the car, nodded thoughtfully at me, and drove off.

I reported in at the camp office. One look at me, and Dad let me off the hook for the day, but added, "I'll need you for the campfire even if we have to make a little one in the shelter. The night hike is on, rain or shine."

I headed for town in lightweight cargo pants and a T-shirt. The warm drizzle soaked me to the skin, but I didn't mind. Maybe I'd drop by the police station and get an update on the search for Francine Dowland. My legs felt heavy, my stomach tight. I let the water wash me clean and kept wondering about Reece. On my way past Florence's, I glanced in, and there was Skid having coffee!

I dashed inside. "What are you doing here?"

"I was boarding to your place when the rain hit."

"Hey, it's just water." I took a seat.

He rested his head lazily against the wall and smiled at me. "She'll be okay."

Heat rose up my neck. "I'm going to buy some rope," I said to change the subject. "Want to come?"

"Sure." He dropped money on the table, and we headed out the door.

I asked, "Are you and your mom going up to Columbus to the hospital?"

"Mom's waiting to see how long Reece'll be in."

"Let me know if you do. I want to go."

I almost expected Skid to razz me, but he didn't. We hung around in the hardware store awhile. He didn't know much about that kind of stuff, so I filled him in on what I knew. I bought all of the rope that I could stuff into my backpack, figuring that I'd give Dad any leftovers to use for the ropes course.

"Let's stop by Mei's," Skid suggested. "We were kind of rough on her last night."

"Okay, but it's still raining. You won't melt, will you?"

"Don't be pushing it, Creek. I'll have to hurt you real bad."

"Yeah, you and what army?"

"United States," he said casually. "I got connections. You'd never know what hit you."

It was fun trading jabs with Skid. It always felt like he saved his best digs for me.

Mrs. Aizawa met us at the door. She bowed but it wasn't a friendly bow. We took off our shoes and wet socks and followed her down the hall. Mei was in the empty den, kneeling before a piece of furniture. Her eyes were closed tight, her hands folded around the crystal, and she was whispering something in dead earnest. When her mother called her name, Mei's eyes popped open. She jumped up when she saw us standing there. "I'm so sorry for my mistake!"

Skid and I practically fell over each other saying, "No, hey, it's cool. We're sorry. It was crazy. No big deal."

She nodded, but she was slumped and sad. "I was

praying," she said, turning to the wooden box. "This is my grandmother's shrine." It was awkward. None of us knew what to say. "I'm praying for Reece to be well."

"You're praying to your grandmother?" I asked skeptically.

"Yes."

Skid gave me a look and said, "My family prayed for Reece last night." He nodded at the picture of her grandmother. "Does she ever talk back to you?"

Mei acted like it was a silly question. She looked at the box with the picture and candles. I couldn't tell if she felt guilty for getting caught praying or about the mix-up at Hermits' Cave or what. There was food in front of the box—a cup of tea and a bowl of rice.

"What's that for?" I asked.

"It's an offering."

"Does she eat it?"

Skid apologized for both of us. "Sorry. We don't know anything about your religion."

Mei seemed embarrassed. "It's our tradition to leave an offering."

"So the food just stays there?" It reminded me of the twins and how they feed the lobbies. Even though the food never goes away, they still believe in them. I didn't say anything, though.

Mei said sadly, "I prayed to stay in America longer so I can be with my friends and get a driver's license."

I swapped glances with Skid. *Stay in America? I thought she was staying longer.*

Mei said, "Let me show you something—a gift I am making." We followed her to her room where she had piles and piles of paper cranes of every color on her bed. What a ton of work. I was impressed.

"It's a custom," Mei said. "One thousand cranes. My mother and sister and brother are helping. We will put them all on strings for Reece to hang in her room. They are wishes for good health."

We hung out in her room a couple of minutes looking at the paper cranes.

I glanced out the window. "Hey, it quit raining. You guys want to go to the next—" Suddenly I saw a spindly spider come crawling out from behind her desk along the baseboard. "Don't look, Mei. I'll get it." I strode over to squash it.

"Don't!" she cried.

I paused, my foot in midair. "It's okay; I'll clean it up." I haven't met a girl yet who'll kill a spider.

"You shouldn't kill it!" she cried.

"You like spiders!?"

"No, but . . . it's bad luck."

Skid's eyebrows went up. "To kill a spider? Whoa, then my luck's shot."

With her bare toe, she scared it back behind the desk, making a yuck face the whole time.

I said, "We have superstitions in America like don't walk under a ladder or break a mirror. Don't step on a crack, or you'll break your grandmother's back."

"It could be the spirit of my ancestor," she said.

Skid and I were struck dumb. We gave each other the you-gotta-be-kidding glance and let it pass.

I changed the subject. "Okay, what say we sweep Cathedral Cave today?"

"Cool," Skid said. "My calendar's free as a bird."

"I can't today," Mei said, looking at the floor to avoid eye contact.

"You have stuff to do?" Skid pried.

"Maybe I need to help my mother cook," she said. "I need to work on the cranes too."

I could tell it was a lie. This wasn't like Mei. She always wanted to come along.

Skid picked up on her mood. "Hey, that's cool. It'd be pretty muddy anyway, wouldn't it, Creek? We can wait. When we go see Reece at the hospital, you want to come?"

"If I can," she said.

The door to the Aizawa house closed firmly behind us, and I muttered to Skid, "You could have cut the tension in there with a knife."

The drizzle started up again as we slogged back to camp. Halfway there I said, "You want to know my deep dark? Let's get Rob and I'll tell you."

I took the guys into Telanoo and showed them my plan.

Skid surveyed the gully and commented in disbelief, "You're building a road?"

"My dad and I did once back at camp," I said. "This won't have to be that good, just enough to get the golf cart all the way to Devil's Cranium."

Rob shoved his hands into his hip pockets. "You can't just put down railroad ties and have a bridge. They'll sink and go all crooked. You have to have a foundation."

"I know that," I said. "I'm deciding how to do it."

He perked up. "Hey, Mom and Dad are having a cement walk poured. I'll watch how they do it."

At long last Skid passed judgment on my deep, dark secret: "Excellent."

Chapter 11

spent the next few hours laying out the first leg of the road. They helped me move big rocks out of the way. We talked about building our own cabin back there sometime. After we'd sawed and hammered forms for the bridge foundation, we dragged ourselves back home. I got dry clothes for everybody, and Mom served soup. "Carlotta called with the Stallards' phone number. You are to call them right away."

I grabbed up the phone and punched the numbers. "Hello, this is Elijah Creek."

"Francine Groves," Dr. Eloise said in a perky way. "She's the owner of the yellowed phone number."

"Francine? Wow. That may be an alias for Dowland's wife."

"Ah, really?" she said surprised. "I understood that she died some years ago."

"Dowland lied," I said.

"What a shame. She must have remarried or taken her maiden name after the unpleasantness."

When Mom left the kitchen, I asked Dr. Eloise if she'd called the Magdeline police about her discovery.

"We wanted to check with you first. We also have her new number."

"Can you hold on a minute?" I covered the phone with my hand and ran this new info past Rob and Skid. They voted for taking it to the police ourselves.

Dr. Eloise said that was fine and for us to stay in touch. "Ms. Groves lives in a little town in Kentucky: Cordova. By the way, since we don't know which language the shoes will have inscribed on them, we are compiling a list of the word *peace* in as many known languages as we can find. We'll send it on when we've exhausted our resources."

"Thanks," I said and hung up. "Can you believe that? They found Dowland's wife before the Magdeline police could."

Skid nodded. "It's a higher priority with them."

Columbus General was the hospital where Dad had taken the poison ivy counselors. When you have as many campers as we do at Camp Mudj, you're going to have injuries, so the ER doctors know Dad by name. I've told him Camp Mudj needs its own parking space at the hospital.

The third day after Reece's surgery, Skid's mom took the four of us to visit her. We got to room 1156 on the eleventh floor, and Carlotta said, "Let me go in first to make sure she's decent."

We waited out in the hall until we got the all clear and went in as a clump. Reece's mom was there, her chair scooted up next to Reece's bed. She was holding Reece's hand and drinking coffee. There were flowers in the window and cards already. I felt bad that I hadn't brought something. Reece was strung up in traction with tubes and machines. It was weird.

"Hey," I said.

Reece beamed at us. We stood back, feeling odd for some reason. She reached out her free hand. "Hey, I'm not toxic!"

Mei bent over and hugged her and gave her a handmade card of paper flowers and gold dragonflies.

"It's beautiful!" Reece said. "Look, Mom. See what Mei made for me?"

Skid said, "She has another surprise for you later. Seriously cool."

Mei said, "It's almost ready. For when you come home."

"Do you want to hear the gory details?" she asked us.

Skid said, "We're all ears."

"Well, after they x-rayed, they found out that the ball of the joint had grown these little barbs. So they put me out and cut me open. They sawed off the top of my leg bone, took it out, and sanded it down. They put it back in with screws and rods and sewed me back up."

I glanced at Mrs. Elliston, figuring Reece was talking out of her head. Mrs. Elliston's nod was matter of fact. "That's exactly what they did. But she came through it just fine." She smiled at Reece. "We have an adventure ahead of us, don't we, sweetie?"

Reece pointed to the windowsill. "Look at my cards and flowers!" The four of us edged around each other like when you're trying to get off a crowded elevator and everyone in front of you isn't getting off until later. We took turns reading the cards, looking at the flowers and reading who they were from, and standing by Reece.

"Relax, guys, will you? I'm not terminal," she said. "Mom, make them lighten up. Those flowers are from my church and my youth group. The daisies are from my dad. He's coming in this weekend. Mom, put Mei's card in the window with the other ones."

No one asked Reece about her future or what kind of "adventure" she'd be facing.

When Carlotta and Reece's mom went out into the hall to talk, Reece gathered us in excitedly. "Guess what? I have to tell you something. Another deep dark I haven't even told Mom yet!" We closed in. "The day I had the surgery, you know? Well, that afternoon the anesthetic wore off, and I started to be in the most awful pain you can imagine. It was the worst I ever had. Ever! They gave me more painkillers that night to help me sleep, but it didn't work. Mom was out in the family waiting room asleep. The nurse said to expect a rough night, but I couldn't stand it. I was all by myself and it was horrible. So I prayed. I said, 'God, I always thought you'd be with us through the valley of the shadow and that you wouldn't give me any more than I could take. I know you can do anything, so please, please be with me and take my pain away, even for a few hours.' Do you know what? Right when I said amen, the pain started to fade, and in one minute it was gone. Just like that." Her eyes misted over. "I always knew he heard and answered prayer, but I never felt it happen like that!"

I wanted to say something, but before I could come up with it, Skid gripped her hand and said, "That's awesome, Reece. That's so cool."

She pulled him down and hugged him hard. "It was more than I could take, so he took it away."

Mei gave her a hug and said that she was happy Reece was feeling better.

Reece said, "I have really missed you, my best friend!" and got emotional.

Rob said, "That's so cool," just like Skid.

I didn't want to say the same as Skid or hug her like Mei with everyone watching, but I couldn't think of anything else, so I shook her hand and blurted out, "Congratulations," like we were closing a business deal. Skid snickered, and I felt dumber than a box of rocks.

On the way back, Carlotta explained more about Reece's condition. "Reece's previous surgery went so well that the bone healed quickly. But, unfortunately, it continued to grow. Little bone spurs have grown out of the ball of the joint and started fusing the bones together. So here's the problem: if Reece gets too little activity the spurs grow, too much activity and inflammation sets in." She sighed and said, "Hm-mm-mm. That little girl has a tough road ahead. When she's older they will probably try to replace the whole joint."

"Until then?" I asked.

"We're all staying positive, doing a lot of praying."

I didn't want to go on searching for the shoes of peace until Reece was good to go. Rob and Mei were in the back seat with me, so while Skid talked to his mom, I asked them in a low voice, "What about the quest?"

Mei sighed. "Long delays possible."

Skid's mom dropped me off at the entrance of Camp Mudj. I took the back road toward Owl Woods around by Morgan's farm. I wanted to be alone. It was late afternoon, and a strong summer wind had picked up. I ran hard, staying to the edge of camp until Great Oak came into view. It felt like forever since I'd been up there. I climbed to the highest branches that would safely hold me, then a little higher until the wind was whipping me around in swirls. The details of Reece's surgery wouldn't have bothered me if they'd happened to a stranger—tough luck and all that.

I couldn't put any of my thoughts together; I looked up to the sky. "If you can take her pain just like that, why can't you take it all away? I'm not smarting off here, but we're trying to find the shoes of peace—and you won't even let her walk." Huge gusts of wind whipped me like I was a rag doll, but I wanted to be heard. I yelled to the sky, "We've had nothing but trouble this whole year! What did she ever do to you!?"

Chapter 12

IT was July by the time Reece got to come home. To keep her involved in the quest, we made her living room our new headquarters. Rob's attic hideout was being redone into a Victorian costume and supply closet anyway, a sign that my childhood was officially over—all the more reason to build a road into Telanoo. Reece's mom had a hospital bed set up next to the front window with all the traction gear and paraphernalia and all her flowers and cards sitting around. Rob and I put the belt of truth and the breastplate of righteousness on a hanger, covered it with a dry cleaning bag, and put it in her closet so we could bring it out for our powwows. Reece kept the maps and Mei's sketches in a shoe box next to her bed where she could get to them anytime. People from her church came out of the woodwork to bring food. Mrs. Elliston was on the phone or at the door saying over and over: "Thanks, dear, but I'm good until November! I appreciate the thought, but people have been so generous. I'm good until November! Thanks, dear, but you should see inside our refrigerator!"

Feeling awkward, I was ready to leave and take Rob with me, when the doorbell rang again.

"Get that, will you?" Mrs. Elliston said.

I opened the door, and there stood a man in khaki slacks

and an oxford shirt, holding a bouquet of flowers. He was light complexioned with short, blond hair and a kind face. For a split second I thought it must be Reece's dad, whom I'd never seen. It took a moment to register because I'd never seen him out of uniform. It was Officer Taylor.

Reece's mom beamed from ear to ear. "Come in, Darrell! Oh, how beautiful!"

He leaned in and handed her the flowers. "For both of you."

There I was getting knocked over by feathers again. Officer Taylor liked Reece's mom?!

"How sweet," she said. "Thank you. Elijah, Rob, do you boys want a sandwich? We could feed a battalion with the food we've been given."

Rob and I hung around and made eye questions to Reece: *What's going on? Did you know? Is this okay with you?*

When Officer Taylor and Reece's mom were out of earshot, she whispered, "I had a deep, dark secret I didn't even know about. How dense am I!"

Rob had to go shopping with his parents for bathroom fixtures, so he didn't stay long. Mrs. Elliston told him, "Take sandwiches and a plate of cookies for your family. We have way too much."

I was ready to take off too when I noticed Officer Taylor grinning at me from the kitchen table. It was weird seeing him out of uniform. I guess I'm dense too, but I had figured he and Mrs. Elliston had been talking about the Dowland case this whole time.

"Elijah here is a resourceful young man," Officer Taylor said. "Has his finger on the pulse of the park and knows it like the back of his hand."

I couldn't tell if he was making fun of me or not, so I just strolled into the kitchen with my sandwich and paper plate. "Did you find out who's making the fires?"

"I'd like to."

"I can see the high spots of Council Cliffs from Devi—I mean from the back of Tel—from that hill I showed you, the one where we found the belt of—where we found that old belt."

He studied me carefully. "Ever been in the park at night?"

"No, sir."

"Do you know it well enough to go in at night without a flashlight?"

Mrs. Elliston stopped what she was doing and looked at him. "You want his help?"

"Right now I'm getting pointers from our local mountain man."

I didn't know what he was getting at. "Full moon or a penlight, that's all I'd need."

He turned to Mrs. Elliston. "Nothing serious has happened yet—that we are aware of. But someone's breaking the law, and it's only a matter of time. The chance for forest fires will increase as we head into the hot, dry end of the summer."

"If you wanted me to go in, I could."

He leaned in, resting his elbows on the table. "We haven't caught these guys because we don't know where to position our officers. The park is spread out with several locations and interconnected roads. There must be several people involved, and they post lookouts. The department doesn't have the manpower to cover all the entrances. These guys move around. Even outfitted with night goggles, our men are just too noisy. You know yourself that once off the path you can't proceed quietly."

"I can," I said.

"So I've heard—from Dom Skidmore." He went on, enthusiasm building in the way he leaned in. "There's no pattern to the fires, except that they're made in restricted areas, either at twilight when smoke and flame are least visible or in the middle of the night when we're low on manpower. By the time we close in, they've run, usually leaving the fires burning."

"What would I be doing?" I asked, trying to keep my manner casual.

"I'm just curious now as to how close you could get without being detected. We need someone who can get near enough to get us an ID—a face and a name. How close could you get?"

"With a light wind to muffle my steps and if the conditions were similar to Farr Island—" I put my hand on his shoulder like I had Skid's that night. "This close."

He looked at Mrs. Elliston.

She smiled. "He is very good at that kind of thing."

"And to stay in contact, I could wear a wire!" I suggested excitedly.

He laughed, then suddenly turned somber. "Don't mention this to your friends, or that's the end of it."

"What about telling Mom and Dad?"

He leaned back and crossed his arms. "We're only talking possibilities, but sure, ask your parents."

"What about Skid and Rob? They trained at Farr Island too."

He studied me skeptically.

"I'll vouch for them!" I prodded. "We know light signals and everything!"

He looked at Mrs. Elliston questioningly. But then she nodded, and that was that.

The twins were at a friend's house, so I mentioned Officer Taylor's idea to my parents at dinner.

"Elijah," Dad warned, "those fires in the park are police business."

"I know, but I could get in there at night, and no one would be any the wiser. Officer Taylor asked me some questions about it."

Mom looked at me suspiciously. "You are not going in there by yourself, I don't care who says so. Those people could be criminals or some kind of satanic cult."

I dipped out green beans. "What exactly *is* a satanic cult?"

"I don't know. People who worship Satan," Mom answered.

"How do you worship Satan. I mean, is that real?"

"Well, *they* think it is."

"But is it?"

Mom said, "Russ, answer your son."

He grinned. "Oh, so he's *my* son when he asks the hard questions." He handed me the rolls. "People can believe pretty crazy things."

"But is Satan real?"

Mom jumped in. "Elijah, I think it's better to say that people make wrong choices than to say that the devil made them do it!"

A strange uncertainty crept over me. "Yeah, I get that. But is he real?"

They looked at each other a long time.

Mom said, "I don't know. If you're a good person, it doesn't matter. You have to find your own truth. Your dinner's getting cold."

I ate in silence for a while, thinking. I really just wanted to know if I could do night maneuvers with the cops, so I put the Satan question on the back burner for the time being. "It wouldn't be dangerous if I were working with the police. I could take a walkie-talkie or wear a wire."

"A wire!" Mom yelped. "Russ, say something!"

Dad sawed away at his pork chop, trying not to look very intrigued. But I know Dad—he was into it.

For me, it would be the coolest thing ever to use my Indian skills and get back in good with the police after looking dumb about the whole empty reject grave mix-up.

After dinner I sat in my room in perfect darkness, drawing room details and shapes of furniture with my eyes, training for night maneuvers. The nagging question was, who were those people in the park? Mitch Bigelow's drug sellers? Was it Francine Dowland, back from the dead and at large, hot on the trail of the armor of God? If it was a satanic cult, what were they doing out there, a short hike from Telanoo?

Other questions simmered gloomily on the back burner of my mind: about God and gods, shrines and Satan, things like that. The uncertainty I'd felt at dinner crept back in; Mom and Dad didn't have the answers. Two of the smartest people in my life didn't know.

The days turned hot and dry. When Officer Taylor called me from the station, I thought the fires in Council Cliffs had reached emergency status and he was calling me in. "You may want to bring your friends over to the station."

"Yeah?" I asked eagerly.

"We have Stan Dowland's wife here."

"You're kidding! You found her? Did she bring the journals? What'd she say?"

"You'll want to hear it from her."

"I'm there!"

Mei wasn't home, so it was the three of us guys. We were ushered into a back room, and there she sat with her purse in her lap and the journals in a stack on the table. She was sort of cut from the same mold as Dr. Eloise with the hair and height and a kind of nervous intelligence, but their faces were nothing alike.

Officer Taylor introduced us as the ones who'd found her daughter's body in the well. We all shook hands and sat around the table in a state of disbelief and awe. It was unreal. For months I'd pictured this woman dead and buried in a reject grave, the mother of Kate, the vanished wife of Stan Dowland, then the elusive journal thief who'd posed as Dr. Eloise. Here she sat in the flesh.

Officer Taylor said to her, "Would you like to tell the boys what you told us?"

Clutching her purse nervously, Francine said, "First I want to thank you for laying my Kate and Adam to rest finally. It's been a loathsome burden. It was good what you did. About Stan, I already told the authorities." Her mouth twitched nervously. "I was there when he died. I guess you could say I killed him."

We three sat stone still as Francine Groves told her story. "I'd been getting the local paper for years under the name Frank Groves, which was my father's name. After what happened at the church those years ago, after I lost my babies, I . . . I had to leave. I couldn't stay in Magdeline. But I wanted to keep up with the news. I cared about people here even though few cared about me. I thought about canceling my subscription many times. A lot of the people I knew from back then were gone; they moved or passed away. I'm so glad I kept taking the paper, or I never would have known about you boys finding Kate and Adam. She was my only daughter, you know. He was my only grandchild.

"It was a shock, reading about it for the first time. It all came back: my broken heart, the secrets and lies." She stopped a minute to catch her breath. Francine Groves may have been the same age as Dr. Eloise, but she had none of the energy and spark. Life had been hard on her.

"I kept up on your story, hoping it would . . . end. I couldn't believe it when they accused poor Bruce. Oh, he was never my favorite person, you can be sure, but his life had been wrecked too, having Kate disappear like that and never knowing where or why. He did love her. I wanted to do something to help him, but I'm ashamed to say I simply didn't have the courage, not even enough courage to come back to Magdeline and tell my side of the story. I handled it like everything else in my life: I sat back and waited, hoping things would work themselves out on their own." She looked directly at us. "That hardly ever works, boys. Learn from my mistakes. More often than not, problems swell and fester; they don't just disappear." She took a tissue out of her purse and blew her nose. "When I saw that Stan was trying to blame Bruce all over again, I got my courage—though it took me a while. I came back, and Stan and I had words in private. It was like no time had passed. We started right back in where we left off, fighting and accusing each other. That's when his heart started acting up. He stormed off to the kitchen to get his medication. I should have stayed to see if he was going to be all right. But I didn't. I walked out the same way I did all those years ago.

"There was no love lost on Stan Dowland, to be truthful, but I take the blame for his death. I shouldn't have left. I could have called for help. I should have—" She broke off and shook her head regretfully. "But I didn't. Can't teach an old dog new tricks."

I asked, "But you did come back for the journals. Why were they so important?"

"Why, the reporter quoted that sappy poem of Stan's right in the paper! I didn't know what kind of hateful things Stan had said about me in those journals. Or about Bruce. Or members of Old Pilgrim Church. He grew very resentful as the years wore on. Never forgave them. I feared the worst every week as I read the paper, just waiting for the other shoe to drop." She paused, her short frame settling even lower in the chair. She went all nostalgic. "I was an educated woman, boys, full of hopes and dreams. How could it all go so wrong?" She sniffed and straightened as if mustering nerve. "It took me a while, but I wasn't going to see my life and my daughter's memory splattered all over the paper for all to read! I came, I *did* come for the journals, ready to spill it all when that woman at the counter mistook me for a Dr.

Stallard." She shook her head and sank back sadly. "It was one more chance for me to slip away unnoticed."

She put her wrinkled hand on the stack of journals. "Here they are. There's nothing in there but poor Stan's useless research and a few personal notes." She paused and eyed us for a minute. "The officer said you boys were looking for the armor."

"Yes, ma'am," I said.

"What do you want with it?"

The less said the better, I thought. "Well, ma'am, we found a piece of it by accident and wanted to find the rest."

"Save yourselves a lot of heartache, boys," she warned. "Stan exhausted himself and wasted years on that armor. It's a troublesome piece of trash. Cost us a trip to Ireland we couldn't afford and became a big part of our financial and marital struggles. Stan got so attached to it that he spent more time studying and looking for—for meaning behind the symbolism than he did the church."

"So you don't know where the rest of it is?" I asked cautiously.

She hesitated. "He buried it somewhere years ago so I couldn't—so no one could get their hands on it. It was magical to him. Silly man."

I was disappointed. "Okay, but I have one more question. The grave," I said. "There was a grave by the church. We thought it was yours."

She smiled a sour smile. "It was."

Chapter 13

I ran right over to Reece's and filled her in about Francine Dowland, aka Francine Groves, aka Frank Groves, alias Dr. Eloise. I hated that Reece had to miss out on meeting Dowland's wife. But she wasn't allowed to move at all for a few weeks, and even then she wasn't allowed to bear any weight, which meant she couldn't walk but only swim. I even got to bring some of the journals for her to read—without a parent's signature, thanks to our insider, Officer Taylor. She was interested in what I had to say for a few minutes, but turned to stare out the window. "Another mystery solved," she said distantly, preoccupied with something else.

"What's wrong?"

She sighed. "It's Mei. When she left yesterday, I said, 'See you soon,' and she gave me the weirdest look. Be sure to let her hang out with you guys, okay?"

I said sure, but the whole idea felt strange. Maybe I'd never stopped thinking of Mei as Reece's shadow. Mei didn't spill her guts about everything like a lot of American girls do. There was a whole bunch about Mei I didn't know.

"Call her," Reece said.

"Okay."

A long pause. "Today," she pushed.

"Okay. We have to sweep the next part of the park. I'll invite her."

Reece took a few minutes to fill me in on Mei's beliefs. "There's lots of superstition in her religion. Her family has gods and rituals and even charms to ward off demons in the house. It's not that she really believes in them, but she doesn't want to bring bad luck on her family if she stops. I know she believes there is a God." Reece sounded desperate. "Elijah, I don't want anything to keep her, or any of us, from finding the armor of God: peace and truth and faith, salvation—all of it."

"I'll do what I can," I said.

"Have fun," she said weakly. She turned to stare out the window again. As I closed the door behind me, I realized it was the first time she'd been left out of the search.

"Moshi moshi," said the voice on the phone.

"Uh, hel . . . lo?" I said.

"Ah, hallo!" It was Mei's mom.

"Is Mei there?"

"Jussa moment."

"Hi, Mei. This is Elijah. Hey, we're doing a sweep of Cathedral Cave. Want to come?"

"I have to ask my mother."

I heard an argument rising up between Mei and her mom in the background. A guy's voice came into the background.

In a few minutes she came back on the phone. "Okay," she said shakily.

"Are you sure?"

"When?" she asked.

I told her where and when.

"I'll meet you there."

"Do you need a ride?"

"I'll meet you there," she said again.

"We can just come by and get you."

"Okay," she said finally.

Rob, Skid, and I stopped by to pick up Mei. Her older brother and sister were sitting barefoot in the mostly empty living room, folding origami paper on the coffee table. Mei introduced us. The brother, Kanta, was a guy version of Mei—taller than her, but shorter than me. His jet-black hair stuck out all over in a cool way and was dyed blonde at the ends. He wore jeans and a white shirt with the sleeves rolled up.

The sister, Yu, had light streaks in her long, feathery hair too, and was wearing a short dress with jeans underneath—kind of weird, but cool.

Mei said, "My sister graduated with a degree in journalism. She wants to translate books. My brother is a sophomore business major." She told them that I helped my father run the nature camp, that Rob was an actor, and that Skid had traveled the world.

Mei's mom came into the living room, smiled, and nodded stiffly at us. She and Mei said stuff back and forth in

Japanese. I didn't understand a word, but it was obviously an argument. Kanta and Yu stopped the paper folding and looked up. They seemed surprised at Mei's nerve.

Rob whispered out of the side of his mouth, "Should we leave?"

Before I could say probably, Mei grabbed her backpack and said, "I'm ready."

I risked a glance at Mei's mom who was glaring at me like I'd tracked in mud.

Mei said, "My mother will pick us up again."

"Um . . . okay," I said uneasily. "Does she know where to come?"

"Cathedral Cave at 7:00. Front entrance."

"There's only one."

Chapter 14

LIKE the rest of the park, Cathedral Cave was formed by water back when the whole state was a shallow sea. At some point thick, vertical slices of rock broke loose from a long cliff, and the base of the slabs slipped out about fifty feet from the foot of the hill. What you get is a cave a block long and forty feet high shaped like a huge upside-down *V* and open at both ends. They call it Cathedral Cave because if you use your imagination, it can look like a Stone Age church. Just when you think you're alone in there, pigeons flap their wings and coo in a low, creepy way from crannies at the top. Bats swoop through at dusk.

People have weddings in there with candles and strings of ivy. But it's full of puddles where the ground dips, and there are always pigeon droppings everywhere, so I don't really get it. People probably use it because we have a shortage of church buildings in Magdeline.

Reece thinks the flood of Noah caused Cathedral Cave. I don't know about that, but it could be. Most Indian tribes have legends of a great flood that covered the earth. Reece said that almost every civilization on the planet has a similar legend, which is a pretty good indication of an actual event. Who am I to say otherwise?

The path to the cave starts at the road and winds up and

down through the woods for a quarter mile until it drops down between two rock monoliths known as Fatman's Squeeze. A huge log spans it at the top. Every time I go down through the squeeze, I look up longingly at that log. What a great place to hang out and secretly watch people go by. I've heard guys dare each other to climb up and cross it, but only a crazy person would try.

I was wondering if the others knew about the secret entrances to the cave, when Mei said, "This is my first time here."

"It's off the beaten track," I said.

"Beaten track?" she asked.

"English cliché alert," Skid said. "What he means is that not many people come to this part of the park. So the track—not like dog tracks, but a path—hasn't been beaten down by lots of feet."

"So many clichés! *Muzukashii,*" she said. "Difficult."

Skid stopped her and took her firmly by the shoulders. "Mei. Hear this. You probably shouldn't be learning English from us. We don't know anything about it. We speak it, but only because we have to."

He joked around with her until she was laughing—the first time in a while. We practiced saying *muzukashii* as we wormed our way through the winding stone steps of Fatman's Squeeze. At the bottom of the steps, the path wraps around the cliff to the left. If you didn't know the cave was there, you might miss it. The giant slab that leans against the cliff looks like the face of the mountainside itself, with deep grooves and breaks in the surface. But the grooves are openings you can slip through to reach the inside.

We let Mei take the lead to see if she would find the secret entrances on her own. We were passing along the base of the cliff when voices came echoing from inside.

Mei stopped and made a sound of surprise.

"Somebody's in there already," I muttered to Rob under my breath. "Dead giveaway."

"Cliché!" Skid scolded. "Try explaining *that one* to her." He shook his head and muttered, "Dead . . . giveaway . . ."

Mei was frightened. "Voices! From where?"

I was thinking, *Well, from people, of course; figure it out.* The fear that flashed across her face surprised me. *What's there to be afraid of out in a public park in broad daylight with three guys to protect you?* I wondered. Maybe she didn't trust us guys with Reece not around. Or maybe it was her religion. There were lots of things to worry about, from what I'd seen and heard: dead ancestors getting angry, people coming back as spiders, demons who had to be kept away by magic charms.

I said to Mei, "Good job! You found the secret entrance! Let's go!"

We squeezed through the wide crack in the stone wall. A family and a handful of college kids were already in there. Little kids were running from one end of the cave to the other; their mom was shouting mom things: "There's a puddle! Don't get your feet wet. . . . Watch the steep drop-off at the end. . . . Slow down, now! Don't go too close. . . . Wait there. Wait for me!"

We did the usual things people do in Cathedral Cave. We ran to opposite ends and waved at each other's silhouettes. We yelled to hear our echoes. Rob followed Mei to the far end and looked out over the cliff.

"There's nothing to see out our side," I told Skid. "The big drop's over there, Lover's Leap."

When we got to the far end, Mei and Rob were at the edge, looking down.

Skid teased, "Let's have no lovers leaping, you kids."

"Shut up," Rob said, but in a minute he was singing a "Twelve Days of Christmas" take-off: "Ten lovers leaping, nine flashlights shining, eight pigeons pooping, seven hikers hiking, six . . . six . . ." He blanked.

Skid jumped to the end of the song, singing flatly, "And a lousy lyric-writer in a cave. Spare us, Wingate."

At the bottom of the forty-foot cliff, the narrow, rocky path wound through the woods beside a sparkling stream. We were eye-level with some of the treetops. No breeze stirred. The woods sat quiet except for birds and the family heading off down the path. Mei asked, "This is Lover's Leap?"

I explained, "If boyfriends and girlfriends can't be together, they come here and jump."

She said, "It's like our Suicide Cliff. It's a beautiful place to die."

"What?!" Rob's shout echoed back through the cave.

"We have a Suicide Cliff in Shirahama, near my hometown. People go there and jump to the rocks in the Pacific Ocean. It's called a beautiful place to die," she said calmly.

"Well, I don't know of anyone who's actually jumped from here, do you guys? They just call it that because it's high and . . ." My voice trailed off uneasily.

"Suicide is very common in Japan," Mei said matter-of-factly.

"Okay, let's get started," I said, steering off the subject. "The cave first. I brought a couple of flashlights. We'll go in pairs. Mei and I will take this end; Skid and Rob, you sweep the other end. Look high and low. Dowland might have picked this place because it's like a church. Don't miss a nook or cranny. Then we'll split up and check out that path."

Rob said cheerily, "Shoes of peace, here we come!"

Skid and I exchanged worried looks above Mei's head.

We checked for stash holes, but no luck. I tried to get Mei to open up about what was wrong, though I figured she was mostly worried about Reece.

"Your brother and sister are cool," I said.

"I'm going to miss my sister. Yu is going to study abroad this fall. Kanta is going back to the university. Our family is going all over the place," she said sadly.

"But you've got *us!*" I joked. "We're a clan!"

We met in the middle of the cave at the secret entrance.

I said to the guys, "Let's separate here; the path out there loops around through the woods. Mei and I will meet you in the middle at the far side."

Mei and I walked along through tall trees, looking for fresh digs. I worked up nerve and asked, "Is . . . uh, is something wrong, Mei?"

She walked on; I didn't think she'd heard me. I was ready to ask again when she opened up. "My mother doesn't trust my friends. I told her that you are good, that you are Christians. But she says that Christianity is a Western religion and that your religion causes wars."

I wished Skid or Reece were here; I didn't know what to say for a while. "Well, what about the Moravian connection? They were Christians who wanted peace. Reece and Skid and their parents, Rob and me, we don't like fighting."

Mei stopped and faced me. Sometimes I compare people to animals. Reece is a canary, Skid's a black cat, Mrs. Otto the town librarian is a lemur. And standing there with a sadness about her and a quiet moan coming from her throat, Mei reminded me of a mourning dove. She said, "I told my mother about your one God, how he took Reece's pain, but she said, 'In Japan we have many gods.'"

"You're not in Japan, Mei; you're in America. But God doesn't just live here. He has power over every country. He can be anywhere."

Her words started gushing out. "My mother is afraid of one God who wants everyone to worship just him. She doesn't want me to be a Christian." She stopped and faced me. "She doesn't trust what I am doing, and she is right. I was never in a police station in my life until I came to America. She is suspicious when I come home and smell like campfire smoke and when we have all stayed together at the lodge. She said American kids do whatever they want, and no one stops them."

This had been coming for a long time.

"When my mother saw my sketches of the armor, I tried to explain about spiritual war . . ." Her eyes welled up with tears. "This is my deep, dark secret, Elijah. My father has signed a contract to stay longer in America, but my parents have decided to send me back to Japan!"

Rob came bounding into view, sweaty and full of energy. "Nothing this way, so we're done! Let's go back and hang out at the cave—" He stopped short when he saw the look on Mei's face.

Skid came up. "We got trouble?"

I was three-fourths through rehashing Mei's problems when she clenched her fists and interrupted me. "I . . . don't want . . . to go!! I don't know what to believe!" She burst into sobs.

We were totally thrown back. Mei was always so mild and agreeable. Skid threw an arm around her neck. "Easy, girl, easy. Not so intense. One step at a time, okay?"

WITH summer sizzling—which meant lots of pool time and water games—you'd think the chaos in my life would have eased up. It didn't—it just moved from outside of me to inside. There was no sign of the raven or Bloocifer, but I felt like they were still out there somewhere—well, Bloocifer, anyway.

I'd pretty much given up on the raven.

The twins traded making weed salad to feed the lobbies in favor of dropping nuts and apple chunks in a path to the house in hopes of catching a replacement for Lady Nibbler. With each new crop of campers, Dad gave stern warnings to the counselors that there be no mention of snakes. Responsibilities would be taken seriously or heads would roll. Because of the dry conditions and the overall laziness of the staff, Dad had me teach them another lesson about fire safety and first aid.

I called them down to the lake and started my spiel. "Okay, we're going to review our wilderness survival skills."

Brad joked, "Oh, like how to eat your young? Been there, done that." The others cackled and it went downhill from there. All I managed was a short lesson on putting out a fire and leaving no trace. I tried to get their interest. "You know, Hermits' Cave is named after two teens who were able to live there secretly for decades because of their survival skills."

"They were teenagers *for decades?*" Brad guffawed.

I was going to tell them how the boys lived off the land and kept it intact, but they kept interrupting and cracking stupid jokes.

"Hey," I defended, "you should know this stuff. Nature provides everything we need!"

Brad huffed. "Yeah, snakes and thorns and poison ivy, deadly heat, pond scum . . . nature stinks."

Yeah, he was dissing nature, but I took it personally and exploded in his face, "Then why'd you sign up for a *nature camp?!*"

He winked at the girls. "The food."

The girls giggled. None of them cared diddly, so I dropped it and told them to get back to work. "And try not to take any more afternoon naps," I said coldly. "They're for babies." As they wandered off for the pool, I said under my breath in a sinister tone, "One of these days, nature's going to take a big bite out of you. Then you'll learn some respect."

Still hoping her parents would change their minds, Mei didn't want us telling her deep dark to Reece. We tried to stay out of trouble and out of the police station for Mei's sake. We sat around at Reece's every few days with our summer reading assignments. Mei took her sketch pad;

I learned to whittle. Rob finished his reading early, so he sometimes relieved Reece when her arms got tired of holding her book while flat on her back. The search for the shoes of peace was on temporary hold.

Reece loaned me her Bible, and I started reading it to find out what made her tick. How could she stay so calm and cheerful most of the time, especially when the rest of the world was out playing and her future—as she always said with a smile—was "up in the air"?

Alone in my room at night with the lights off so I could train my eyes, I often chewed over Mei's comment that I could be trusted because I was a Christian. What did it mean to be a Christian? Was I one? I agreed with Reece that there was one big God, but Mei's mom was right about one thing too: it was a scary idea. I decided, though, that having lots of little gods that you carry around in boxes and old folks who might come back as spiders wouldn't be a whole lot of comfort when things got tough. I decided to stay with one big God who knows how to run the world and the weather and all the universes in space all by himself. But I still wasn't sure—not as sure as Reece and Skid.

One such night when I thought on deep things, it occurred to me that the place opposite of peace wasn't just Indian war council sites, but inside my own self.

As August approached, the four of us worked on the road and bridge but kept the project from Reece. It was to be the deepest, darkest secret of the summer. When Reece was up and around again, we'd stage a surprise powwow on Devil's Cranium.

It was a lot of work. Everyone had his or her specialty. Skid and I scouted ahead and kept the road heading in the right direction according to Rob's map. Rob kept tabs on the weather forecasts and took charge of the bridge foundation. When Mei was allowed to come, she drew landmarks on the map and tagged the trees. Once we had the direction of the road, we started putting up permanent markers section by section and clearing rocks. Sometimes Mei brought a big lunch in a stack of black and gold Japanese boxes, which she tied up in a big scarf. In each box she'd have something different: rice balls, fruit, cake. I'd have been okay with peanut butter, but Mei liked making fancy dinners, using the scarf as a tablecloth spread on a rock. I always brought a jug of water and hung it from a tree. We guys opened the spigot right into our mouths. Mei used a cup.

No one said much over the next few weeks; we saved our energy for the work. But inside we all were thinking how surprised Reece would be when we drove her all the way up to Devil's Cranium to see the view: the meadow, the farms, and the hills of Council Cliffs. I knew that's what we were all thinking by the way we'd stop to get a breath and look where we were headed and not complain about the heat or our cuts and bruises.

The flat sections of the road went fast. All we had to do was tag trees and clear branches. Other places were back-breaking, the hardest work I'd ever done, harder than when my Dad and I built the road to the maintenance building—because we had no equipment with this road, and I was in charge this time. Wherever our road crossed a gully, we stacked flat stone across in two wide tracks. I knew that the first big downpour might wash out the rocks, but it would do for now. We got Uncle Dorian to dump off his scrap lumber by the maintenance building. Between that and the scraps from the Tree House Village and stuff I bought with my summer money, we had all we needed for the bridge.

By the time we were on the last big section of the road, I was doing sunrise duty at camp, working off and on through the day, then campfire and cleanup in the evening. By night I'd fall into bed worn out. I was driven to get that bridge and road done. Looking back, I think I believed that once the project was finished, Reece would be well, Mei's parents would have changed their minds, and we'd all be starting another year of school together.

We finally reached the incline to Devil's Cranium on a hot Saturday at twilight. I sprinted up to the summit ahead of the others to measure how much daylight we had. That's when I spotted the fire at Hermits' Cave. At first I thought it was the sunset reflecting on something in the distance, but as the sky lost color, the orange speck on the heights got brighter. There we stood on Devil's Cranium, the dying sun to our backs, an unlawful fire flickering in the distance.

Rob reached the summit and read my mind. "We're not supposed to go in after dark by ourselves."

I knew that, but the fire was calling to me. I was ready to scamper down that big, old, skull-shaped hill and make a beeline past the ruin and Kate Dowland's well and straight for the park.

Skid came up beside me. "By the book, Creek."

"Okay. Let's go."

Chapter 16

✻✻✻

I was the first one back to camp. I called Officer Taylor and then started working on Mom. "Dom Skidmore told the police I was the best he'd ever seen! I could get in there at night, and no one would be any the wiser. It's just like Farr Island—we'd have people looking out for us. Skid and Rob will go too!"

Mom shook her head, "I can't see Dorian and Grace agreeing to a scheme like—"

"Dom can explain it to them," I said as I punched numbers on the phone and asked Carlotta to tell Dom to call Uncle Dorian 'cause we had to move on this now. Then I followed mom around the kitchen, pleading my case like a hungry puppy.

She pulled something great-smelling out of the oven and huffed. "You're not going in there by yourself! They could be criminals or who knows?"

The doorbell rang.

I headed for the door, calling back, "He'll explain it all. It wouldn't be dangerous if I were working with the police. Can I ask Dad?" I flung the door open. "Officer Taylor!"

He stepped in. "I was two minutes away."

I let him in and headed back to the kitchen. Dad and Skid came in at the same time. By the time Rob showed up,

I'd rushed through what we did at Farr Island and how we could use our skills for Hermits' Cave.

In a matter of minutes, Dad and Officer Taylor shook hands. (Dad stifled a proud grin. He was eating this up.) Then Rob, Skid, and I were on our way. Mei came huffing in. As I dashed out, I asked Mom to take her home.

On the way to the park, it struck me how we were using all the things we'd learned. It was like my life was becoming a series of questions and answers: *Why is this happening?* I'd ask. Then the reason would become clear. Like I was living out some kind of well-orchestrated plan.

We'd know what we were doing tonight only because of Farr Island and because we'd worked out a light code with Donovan when we searched for the breastplate of righteousness at Theobald's. Officer Taylor had okayed us only because we had Dom Skidmore's seal of approval.

I had already made contingency plans for every site and laid out my Hermits' Cave plan for the three of us: Cong, Viking, and me, Navajo. "I'll go the east rim trail, you guys stay in the gorge. Skid, you keep an eye out for lookouts on the east rim; Rob, you're in charge of watching the side trails and keeping an eye on the west rim. Always stay beneath me so we can signal each other."

"You're doing the rim trail with no light?!" Rob questioned.

"Yeah."

"All those broken off places?"

No one should run the rim trail at night if they don't know every dip and turn. Some shadows are shadows, some are empty space. One false step and . . . I held up my fist to Rob. "Back of my hand."

Once in the park, we stood in darkness at the head of the trail. The police taped wires on all three of us. We were dressed in black and had penlights, and high-powered flashlights tucked in our belts just in case. Officer Taylor and park security had guns. Cruisers were posted at both entrances: Hermits' Cave and Eagle Rock Falls.

"I'll signal Skid and Rob if I see anything; they'll alert you guys," I told the security team. "If I'm close to the campfire, I won't talk into the wire and risk blowing my cover." I told Skid and Rob, "If I disappear, don't worry. Maintain your positions in the shadow and keep your eyes and ears on high alert."

"How long will it take you to get to the site?" asked one of the park team.

"No more than twenty minutes once I reach the rim trail, but if you don't hear from me in thirty, don't try to communicate. I'll need all my senses focused on the dark."

We worked our plan based on my knowledge and Rob's map of the site. They were a little suspicious of why Rob had detailed layouts of the park, but Officer Taylor told them we were treasure hunters and gave them a wink. We still had the benefit of people thinking we were just kids. It was great cover, and even though we were civilians, they treated us with a lot of respect and gave us encouragement.

"You know exactly where the fire is?" Officer Taylor asked.

"Almost positive. Northeast of the cave on the rise before you cross over into Eagle Rock Falls territory. On an outcropping of rock that makes a flat spot. It's surrounded above on two sides by short cliffs. A good place for a fire—sheltered and half hidden. I could see diffused light from Devi—from my hill near camp. It was fire reflecting off those cliffs. I'm almost sure of it."

"Let's do it," Officer Taylor said.

I added, "There's a good tree this side of the outcropping. I might climb it for a better vantage point, or I might circle around the short cliff and creep up on them from above."

"Be careful," Officer Taylor said, tipping his head in an official way at me.

I pulled my shoes off. "They'll never know I'm there."

Skid and Rob followed me into the park, lights off.

In one way it was about the creepiest thing I'd ever done. These weren't boo hag dummies with plastic eyes and fake blood—they were real live troublemakers. In another way it was the coolest yet. Night maneuvers!

"Take it steady and don't make noise," I told Skid and Rob. "If you get off the path, test each step." We split up.

I sped along the rim trail, my feet feeling the cool dirt and dodging twigs and leaves on the path. For an instant I was a young Delaware brave, running for my life, quiet as moonlight, heart pounding like a sacred drum. Somewhere ahead in the dark were my enemies—encroaching on my land, never to be trusted.

I'd made it almost to the ledge above the bridge where Reece had gone down; Skid and Rob had followed below me in the canyon like a double shadow, taking cues from my moves. Up the hill in the distance, ahead and to my right, was a dull orange glow broken into faint, tiny pieces by the trees—exactly where I thought it would be. I figured if the enemy had a guard, he'd be posted below the flat spot, maybe another one above on the short cliff.

I signaled quickly with the penlight for the guys to hold their positions until I'd scouted it out. The trickling stream down in the gorge had almost dried up from the hot summer, which could work to our advantage or not. I might hear the enemy better, but they might also hear me. My eyes were wide as a raccoon's, alerted for a sneak attack, wary of a deadly shove off the ledge. I called on my night vision like never before.

The coast seemed clear. I turned to signal the guys, hoping they could make it up one of the crevices we'd seen on our earlier expedition. We'd stake out on the overhanging ledge, and I'd move on up the hill . . . but something was moving down there, something behind them. Skid and Rob's attention was on me; they had no idea it was behind them . . . an oval shape, large and lumbering, moving through the gorge toward them. It wasn't human, it wasn't a cloud shadow over the moon. It wasn't a dog . . . my mind flashed back to answering Reece about the dangers in the park: *I've heard that black bears are making a comeback, but I've never seen one myself.*

Of course . . . hot weather . . . lack of water in the hills . . . the cool gorge stream . . .

The bear didn't show alarm, didn't seem to know Skid and Rob were ahead of it. If I signaled retreat, Skid and Rob would turn and run right into it. If I pointed out the bear, the city boy and the history-buff-turned-sky-watcher would freak. The mission would be compromised.

Suddenly the bear stopped. It spotted them.

I had no choice. "Bear!" I said into the wire. Then I pulled the high-powered flashlight out of my belt, flipped it on, and beamed it down into the face of the big black bear.

I waved my arm, yelling at the guys, "Don't move!" while running back along the rim to distract the bear and scare it away from them.

The guys turned and froze in place.

Disoriented and startled by my flashlight and the commotion above it, the bear turned tail and ran. He loped down the path a few yards, took a sudden right, and vanished among the trees.

I yelled down, "Make sure he's gone; then go! Go!" I signaled with the penlight to confirm my orders: retreat. Then I said into the wire, "Lights on! Head into the gorge. We have a bear!"

Skid and Rob took off, halting every few yards to scan the woods with their flashlights. I spun around to check for surprise attacks from anything or anybody on the rim trail. *All clear.* I heaved a sigh. I'd probably blown our cover, but what else could I do?

Up on the hill the fire still glowed strong.

Maybe . . . maybe they hadn't heard.

Swift and quiet as I could, I flew up the hill. My plan was to storm the camp. I'd start yelling, "Bear! Bear in the woods!" This would throw them into chaos; I could make an ID and get out. They'd never catch me, and I'd have a description, maybe a name.

When I looked up again to get my bearings, the fire was out. I stopped short, listened. The stream was a faint echo behind me. Ahead, dead quiet. Slowly I crept around the base of the short cliff, following my nose up to the flat spot. It was vacated and dark. The smell of smoke was strong in the air. I dropped on one knee and felt around on the ground. Sure enough, a hot spot. But there was no sign of a fire. This time they'd left no trace.

By the time I returned to the rim trail, a train of lights was bounding down the lower path in my direction. I whooped to signal my location. The lights gathered seventy feet below and made a beam that came together on me. I was in the spotlight, literally.

"I'm okay! Coming down."

I apologized for ruining the operation. The park authorities were hesitant to believe us about the bear, but they followed its path up the hill and found a set of tracks. One of the security guys said, "This kind of thing is happening more often because of the bear repopulation. In May one came out of the woods behind Armstrongs' house, ran down the yard, and crossed the highway."

I explained how I found the site still warm and smelling of smoke but with no trace of a campfire. "You say they leave the fire burning, they leave the ashes?" I asked.

"Always," said Officer Taylor.

"Well, they didn't this time."

Officer Taylor sighed. "They're getting smarter."

Yeah, I said to myself, starting to steam, *smarter—or better educated.* A picture formed in my mind of a bunch of irresponsible poison ivy patients whom I'd just taught to make a fire without leaving a trace.

On the way back in the cruiser, I said to Rob and Skid, "See if you can stay over tonight."

Officer Taylor dropped us off at the camp, and after we told the whole story to Mom and Dad, we went to my room. I checked in on the twins to make sure they were asleep before I laid out my plan. "Rob, do you have any stage makeup at your house?"

"Yeah. Why?"

"Stuff to make scars?"

"Yeah."

"Can your mom bring it over tomorrow?"

"I guess so. Why?"

I turned to Skid. "I need you to borrow Reece's wheelchair. Have your mom bring it over tomorrow morning."

"What's cookin'?" he asked.

I grinned. "A smokeout."

Chapter 17

THE next morning I went early to Dad's office and explained my plan.

He was quiet for a long time, but I could see the gears turning behind his eyes. "Are you absolutely sure?" he asked.

"Ninety-nine percent."

His face went to fury. "Did you tell the park authorities this?"

"No, because . . . Camp Mudj's reputation is at stake."

"You think we should handle it . . . quietly?" he asked.

"It's best for the camp. Rob can do it. You know he can."

Ever so slowly he started to grin. "I'll disavow all knowledge . . ."

"Okay by me. He can be ready in an hour."

Dad was just starting the camp counselors' meeting at the gazebo when Carlotta pulled into our driveway. She had on sunglasses and was holding a mug of hot tea. I went up to her window. "Is everything a go?" I asked.

She lifted her sunglasses at me and grinned. "All systems go. I'm hiding behind this tea because I will not be able to keep a straight face. Good luck."

Lights, camera, action.

I jogged over to Dad's staff meeting, my face in a

concerned frown. "I'm sorry, Dad, but we need help getting Rob into the house."

"Sure," he said seriously. "Brad, you and Ramsey. Actually let's all go over and say hi. Rob needs cheering up. We had a near tragedy last night."

Skid got out of the back seat of his mom's car, unfolded the wheelchair, and wheeled it around to the passenger side. Just as the counselors got to the driveway, Skid opened the door with a dramatic sweep. Their faces went slack. Painfully, Rob eased himself out of the car. He was in shorts and a bloody, torn T-shirt with thick bandages on his right hand and left thigh and a wrapped belly. One eye was swollen black and blue. I said, "We can wheel him to the bottom of the steps, but it'll take three of us to carry him up."

"What happened!?" one of the girl counselors asked.

I'm not an actor and neither is Skid, so we just let Rob take over. He leaned his head back and peered at her pitifully from under his swollen eyelid. "Bear attack."

Once we got him up on the porch (he did the best groans and grimaces you ever heard), he told how there were illegal fires burning in the park, how the townspeople were sure there were satanists in there and were fed up with it. They were talking a vigilante shoot-to-kill mission. His voice went as old and crackly as the Romeos' as he quoted the vigilantes: "We'll blow the fool heads off those devil worshipers!" Rob explained that the police had to take action before someone got murdered. He paused to catch his breath, acting as if telling the story exhausted him. "So they called on Elijah because he knows the park better than anyone in the state. They knew he could find whoever was starting the fires. So . . ." Rob grimaced as he painfully put his feet on the wheelchair footrests, then went on: "The police were going to close in as soon as they got the word from Elijah. Skid and I had gone in too," he added humbly, "because of our jungle military training. I was scouting ahead down a west path, when all of a sudden I came face-to-face . . . with a big, black bear."

I dared a glance at Brad; he was buying every word of it. How could he not? My cousin's a genius actor.

Rob told in horrific detail how the startled bear attacked him, taking swipes at his gut to disembowel him and how one diagonal swipe had gashed him from right to left. How he'd screamed for help, but we were scattered in all directions; how the bear had gotten its teeth lodged into his eyebrow and was fixing to eat out his eyeball when help came.

There on the porch, surrounded by the worst set of counselors we'd ever had, Rob peeled back his belly bandage, showing just enough of the bloody claw swipes to make the girls cover their mouths and the guys stare in horror. How he could conjure up real tears while Skid and I were biting our lips numb to keep from busting out, I'll never know. Skid turned away and shoved his hands into his pockets as if revolted by the sight of the bloody scars. Rob never fell out of character. Even when one of his fake wire stitches fell off, he just grabbed at his stomach to cover, caught his breath, and went on about how he was probably still bleeding internally.

"That bear could have rabies," Rob moaned. "The doctors said if they don't find him, I might have to have a whole lot of shots into my stomach . . . right here!" He peeled back the bandage over the claw marks once more. (I had thought this was a little over the top when we rehearsed the night before, but Rob convinced me he could pull it off.) "They shot at the bear as he ran off," he said finally. "One cop swore he wounded it, but we don't know. So there's a good chance a wounded bear is still on the prowl in Council Cliffs State Park. They might close the park. That bear has tasted my blood, and he's hungry for more."

He weakly thanked Brad and Ramsey for the help with his wheelchair, then turned and looked up at me pitifully. "I need to rest now." I stopped breathing and curled my toes from the strain of trying to keep a straight face.

The counselors wandered back toward the gazebo, muttering under their breaths. I was sure we'd seen the end of the "satanists" in the park and the last of the poison ivy.

Before we could even get Rob wheeled over the threshold, Skid and I were snorting like pigs. Once inside the door, Rob rolled out of his wheelchair, started peeling off scars and throwing them around. I dropped to the floor and curled into a ball of belly spasms. I thought I'd die laughing—for real.

Chapter 18

IT was mid-August. Summer camps were winding down. One night after dinner, I joined Dad out on the porch. The moon was up, and crickets chirped. The cabins were empty, the counselors off for the weekend. The fires in Council Cliffs had mysteriously ceased.

I plopped down in a rocking chair. "I guess Bloocifer's a lost cause. Haven't seen anything of him."

Dad just nodded.

"You know what I think?" I went on. "I think the counselors were fooling around and let him loose."

Dad said thoughtfully, "If I had it to do over, I would have re-staffed for the summer. But it's so hard to get good help." He paused. "Bloocifer was a nice addition to the nature center. Blue racers are hard to come by—too aggressive."

Down beyond the lake, a ring of luminaries glowed around the wildflower meadow. A string of people with candles were making their way down to the lake and around the meadow one by one.

"What's that?"

"A retreat group on a prayer walk."

"What's a prayer walk?"

Dad said, "I guess it's where you pray—and walk. Oh, that's something you can do for me: tomorrow morning could you go around the perimeter of the meadow and pick up their prayer signs and luminaries?"

"The guys are coming over first thing. We were going to hang out."

"It'll only take a few minutes. You know where the luminaries are stored. Use the wheelbarrow to gather them. The signs and stakes you can pitch."

Candles floated around the meadow. People were singing softly. I felt my whole body sink down into the rocker. It was so peaceful. "Dad?"

"What, son?"

"What do you believe about God?"

A long pause. "I think there's someone up there."

"Aren't you curious about what he's like?"

He kind of chuckled. "I hardly have time to think about anything but business."

For some reason his answer really annoyed me.

"Reece said that after her surgery, she was in this awful pain, and she prayed and the pain went away—just like that. She said it was God."

"Hmm."

"I think there's something to it."

"Maybe so."

Next morning at sunup and pushing a wheelbarrow, I followed the trail of signs and luminaries. I pulled up one sign, thought about it, and then moved on to the next.

GOOD EVENING, FATHER, the first sign said. *Good morning, . . . Father,* I said toward the sky.

CREATION SINGS YOUR PRAISE. *Well, yeah, birds are going crazy in the trees. The mist is rising off the lake.*

I KNOW YOU ARE HERE, the third sign said. *Well, I'm talking to you, so I hope you're listening. Hey, remember when the tornado was coming and everybody was screaming up the stairs at me? I heard when you whispered, "It's okay. Go." I heard that.*

FIVE THINGS I AM GRATEFUL FOR ARE . . . *I don't know—lots of things. My family, the quest, Reece and Rob, Skid and Mei, Camp Mudj, that's more than five . . .*

THERE ARE THINGS IN MY LIFE I CAN'T HANDLE, LORD . . . I pulled up the sign and dropped it in the wheelbarrow. *I don't know. Well, the quest. I mean it's going okay. I'm not complaining, but we always have problems finding the pieces. Sometimes I wonder why you're making it hard. And the whole thing with Reece. And Mei. I'm a little worried. Am I supposed to do something about that?*

I GIVE THOSE TO YOU. *What? The problems? I'm supposed to turn those over?*

I KNOW I CAN DO ALL THINGS THROUGH CHRIST. *Okay, this is over my head.*

FORGIVE ME AS I STOP HERE AND FORGIVE OTHERS. *I can't think of anyone right now that I'm ticked at. I hope that's okay. Rain check. And about you forgiving me, well, that lying stuff a few months back . . . see, I'm over that. But if there's anything else I've done . . . just let me say that I've seen your work, and I don't ever want to get on your bad side.*

COME QUICKLY, LORD! I pulled up the last sign, wondering if people really do want him to come quickly. *Isn't that the same as wanting the Day of Evil to come?*

IN THE NAME OF JESUS, THE ETERNAL ONE, AMEN.

Hey, I've just done a prayer walk. A big, warm feeling swelled in my heart, and in a flash I understood why Reece looked so calm and happy when she prayed. I looked across the lake at the lodge, its windows blazing with the reflection of sunrise, more sunlight sparkling through the trees. On my porch Dad was drinking coffee and writing on his clipboard. A feeling of peace welled up in me that I can't describe. Skid and Rob would be here in a few minutes, and we'd work on our road. The land no one owned would soon be my own private wilderness forever. Life was good.

I was cutting across the meadow when I spotted something, and my mind suddenly cleared of everything but one word: *Bloocifer.*

Cobra-style he was arched up, looking at me above the tall grass with his cold, black, Egyptian eyes. Slowly I set the wheelbarrow down. I could yell for Dad, but Bloocifer would run or strike for sure. Racers don't like humans, and if snakes have memories, Bloocifer for extra sure didn't like me.

I had no weapon, but I had to have that snake.

I'll storm him. I'll just rush him. He'll lunge; I'll swing around and grab him behind the head. So what if he bites? It'll hurt and that's all. The teeth will break off, and I'll have him. Whatever he does, I'm still faster. Four miles an hour? Eight? I can do that. Wait. He lunges faster than he slithers. I do need a weapon.

He hadn't moved. He was so stone still, I wondered for a moment if he was fake, a rubber snake Dad had planted there as a joke. I looked up at the porch. Dad wasn't looking. He had too much on his mind for pranks. This was no joke. Bloocifer wasn't moving. *Why?* I moved in carrying the COME QUICKLY, LORD! sign as my only defense.

"Hey!" came a voice from above. It was Rob, with Skid behind him, barreling down the hill. I put up both hands—still carrying the sign—but they didn't get it was a signal to stop. *What do I do, what do I do?* I wanted Bloocifer; it was a matter of principle. Rob was still barreling around the lake path when he caught sight of the blue racer and came to a screeching halt. Skid piled up behind him.

I was twenty feet away from Bloocifer, figuring my best bet was to rush him. Heart pounding, I rushed forward ripping off my T-shirt and whirling it around my right arm to make a guard against his fangs. Bloocifer stood his ground until I was almost on him, then he lunged for me. For a split second we were airborne—him lunging and me leaping to the right to dodge him. He hit the ground a yard past where my feet had been. I spun to face him, back-stepping toward the lake. Something else caught my eye in the grass to my right, a writhing pile of black and white. *What in the world?!*

Baby racers! A nest of little speckled babies was a yard from my feet! I went up on one toe, leaped away, my eyes darting to see where Bloocifer had gone. "He's a she! He's a she!" I screamed. A flash of blue to my left. Bloocifer was coming back for me. In a fury she lunged again. I swatted wildly at her with the sign. The whack threw her back, but only for a second. I had to make a quick decision. I threw the sign at her, scooped up two handfuls of baby snakes and took off toward the lake path.

"Babies!" I yelled, speeding toward Rob. He did a double take, saw the squirming wad of snakes in my hands, and tripped sideways toward the lake to get out of my way. I heard a splash and a squeal behind me as I sped on toward Skid, yelling, "Bloocifer's mad! Run! Run!"

Skid spun and shot up toward the lodge. Behind me was splashing, screaming, and then feet pounding pavement. I ran full throttle for the nature center with a handful of writhing baby blue racers and Bloocifer somewhere behind me in the grass. "Daaaad!"

I wondered if I'd ever camp out again.

I was checking up on Reece when Mei came by with the biggest pile of paper birds you ever saw. They were every color of the rainbow and some silver and gold. They were strung on long pieces of fishing line and gathered in a knot at the top. It was as pretty as a bouquet of flowers but a whole lot bigger.

Reece squealed and went on and on.

Mei said, "They mean a thousand wishes for your good health."

Reece's mom came into the living room and went through the same little fit of excitement. She and Mei hung them up from a plant hook in the ceiling at the head of Reece's hospital bed where she could touch them. The birds hung almost to the floor. Reece spun them in the light, and the gold and silver ones sparkled. "This is the most beautiful thing anyone has ever made for me. How many hours did it take?"

"My family helped me."

"Really? Tell them thanks. But how long? Days, I bet. Mei, you're the best friend I've ever had! I'll keep this forever!"

Mei's eyes fell to the floor.

Uh-oh, I thought, *here it comes.*

Reece said, "Mei, what's wrong? I'm doing really good. I'm swimming almost every day. I'll get to go to school and—"

Mei covered her face. Mrs. Elliston put her arm around her. "What's the matter, sweetie? Reece is going to be fine. We're taking good care of her."

Mrs. Elliston sat Mei down on the couch and gave her a tissue and nodded me over to sit down beside her. What was I supposed to do? But I went over anyway and sat like a knot on a log. I took a deep breath. "Your deep dark?"

Mei's head nodded in her hands. "But I can't say it."

Reece said, "Come here, Mei. You can tell me. We can tell each other anything."

Mrs. Elliston brought a chair over from the kitchen. Mei sat next to Reece's hospital bed and told her deep dark in broken words. "I have to go back to Japan soon. I don't want to go. I prayed to God, but he didn't answer me. I hope the wishes I made for you don't bring you bad luck."

Without a word Reece reached for Mei's hand, and they knotted fingers. Mei laid her head down on their knotted hands. They closed their eyes and cried.

Reece's mom slipped into the kitchen and turned on the light. The sun was going down, and the picture window was gold and orange with clouds. I sat there on the couch and watched the sky get orange. Mrs. Elliston motioned for me to come into the kitchen. She filled a glass with ice and poured a cup of hot tea over it. The ice crackled.

I sat at the kitchen table, and she sat close beside me, patted my back, and whispered. "We have to let them grieve."

I slugged down the tea and watched the sunset fade. "How can God do this? I don't get it," I said to Mrs. Elliston.

"What, hon?"

"Why is this happening?"

"You pray. He decides."

"It's not fair," I kept my voice low. "It's the worst possible time."

She chuckled a little. "He often chooses the worst possible time. Life's an adventure, Elijah. And adventures are never easy. If they were easy, they wouldn't be adventures, would they?"

I looked over at Reece and Mei crying in the sunset with the thousand birds slowly turning in the sun.

"It looks like a thousand and one prayers unanswered, doesn't it?" Mrs. Elliston said. "But it isn't."

There was still some light left, I thought, feeling detached. *I can finish the road. And if I take a lantern, I can work even longer into the night.*

Chapter 19

A couple of days passed. Mei didn't come around. We figured she was packing her things.

Skid, Rob, and I were helping the Wingates clean up the debris from the last of The Castle's renovations when Aunt Grace came to the front door and called out, "Is Mei with you boys?"

"No."

She came out to the edge of the porch. "Her family is looking for her."

Aunt Grace kept looking at us. "She's not with us, Mom," Rob said.

"Mrs. Aizawa's other daughter is on the phone. They're very upset." Aunt Grace cleared her throat. "Mei left a note."

We put our stuff down and went to the porch. Skid asked uneasily, "What kind of note?"

"It said she's not going back to Japan. Do you know where she might be?"

I didn't want to say I had an idea. "Did they check with Reece?" I asked. "Mei could be at her place."

"Reece said to ask you. Boys, if you know something, now's the time."

I said, "I might know."

Aunt Grace careened into the parking lot at Cathedral Cave, scattering gravel. We piled out and started running. Another car pulled in behind us. It was Mrs. Aizawa, Kanta, and Yu. Skid popped me on the shoulder. "Go on. We'll catch up!"

I flew along the path with Mei's words ringing in my head: *a beautiful place to die, a place to die. Don't do it, Mei! It's not worth it. Don't be there.* I thought of all the places she should be: at Reece's doing summer reading, at Florence's with us eating fries, working on the road through Telanoo. It was strange how her life started flashing before my eyes: that first time we sneaked into Old Pilgrim Church, working backstage on Rob's play, her sketching the armor the first time, digging the belt of truth out of Devil's Cranium, our trip to Chicago with her buying postcards and us eating high-class at the top of the town, and giving Skid grief over his height fright, all the powwows at camp, the quick meetings at my locker. Mei was a huge part of my life, quiet and creative and never any trouble. I hadn't thought about it much until now—how her being gone would wreck the clan. Looking back over the summer, I realized Mei hadn't left many clues. She'd been her usual nice, cooperative self. But all that time she'd been harboring worries about having to leave Magdeline, hoping it wouldn't happen. Arguing with her parents who thought we were filling her head with weird ideas and getting her into trouble with the police. Secret meetings, suspicious archaeologists, empty graves. Runaway snakes and rumors of devil worshipers and forbidden fires. Mei was afraid of bad luck and maybe pondering suicide all along as things got worse. Everything in her heart had been a deep, dark secret.

I slithered through Fatman's Squeeze fast and wheeled left toward the cathedral. To my right a wandering creek, to my left the path to the cathedral, thick tall trees ahead, the narrow walls of the squeeze rising behind me. *Go, go, go,* I told myself. But I couldn't move. What was stopping me? My feet seemed planted. My instincts were telling me something, but what? What was I missing? My eyes darted around, then up . . .

She was above my head, sitting on the log stretched between the high-standing stones, her hand gripping the log.

I didn't call Mei's name because she saw me already.

We looked at each other. Mei raised herself up off the log. I shook my head and held my breath. *No, Mei.*

We looked at each other. "I'll come get you," I said. She paused. "I'm coming."

In a moment she nodded and backed up toward the rock. I headed back up through Fatman's Squeeze as she kept backing off the log toward the cliff.

By the time her family got there, she was by my side.

"She came out here to think," I told them, "and she lost her way."

I didn't lie. It was the absolute truth.

Reece tried calling Mei for the next few days, but her sister said she couldn't come to the phone. I even wondered if her parents had sent her back to Japan without letting her say good-bye. A million things ran through my mind about the clan and the armor, about Reece losing her best friend, and about trusting gods in boxes when your world falls apart.

Then Reece called me and said, "Mei's coming over. Can you guys get here?"

"What's up?"

"I don't know. Just come."

We gathered at Reece's, but we didn't exactly know why. So we sort of sat around and looked at each other. Reece had nothing to say. I was afraid that if I opened my mouth, something supremely dumb would spill out.

"Hey, guys," Rob started reluctantly, "I want to set the record straight."

"What record?" Skid asked.

"I didn't try to commit suicide last spring at Farr Island. I wasn't trying to drown myself."

"Looked like it," Skid said glumly.

"I know." He squirmed. "I won't say I didn't think about it. I wanted to hurt my dad like he was hurting me, and I knew that would do it. But the big reason I went out there in the waves was to blow off steam and cuss and say anything I wanted where nobody could hear me. It was stupid."

He was telling us this now, I figured, because he could see how bad it had looked from the outside. "And I don't think Mei was really going do it. She was probably throwing a fit because her parents are sending her back. I can't see her . . . going through with it."

Reece said, "When she comes, just be nice. Don't embarrass her or make her feel bad."

When Mei got there, we were stiffer than at Aunt Grace's high tea.

Reece held out her hand. "How are you, Mei? Come sit with me."

She rushed over to Reece and grabbed her hands. "I'm sorry to cause so much trouble!"

"No trouble," Skid said casually. "Friends hang tight."

"I am ashamed!" Then she told us all what she'd told me at Cathedral Cave weeks before. "I must leave. My parents are worried that I will get into trouble. If I stayed, I wouldn't be allowed to be part of your clan anyway."

"It's your clan too!" Reece said.

"I went up on that log to see if I could be closer to God. I thought about not coming back. I thought it was a beautiful place to die. But then I thought about what Reece said about her pain: 'It was more than I could take, so God took it away.' I hoped he would take this away, that I'd be able to stay. But my father has bought my plane ticket and asked my aunt to enroll me in my cousins' school. I said to God, 'You didn't answer my prayer. I can't stay. I have no reason to go back. My friends are here. My family is here. I will have no one. So this is the end if you don't stop me.' When I opened my eyes from the prayer and looked down, there was Elijah. God answered my prayer." Tears ran down her face.

Reece said, "God always answers."

Skid added, "But it won't be what you expect. Never is."

Mei said, "It's best that I go, but it's not what I want."

Chapter 20

BECAUSE I'd helped the Aizawas find their daughter, they felt indebted and agreed to let us have one final powwow. Reece had graduated to her wheelchair. We took the golf cart into Telanoo and across Shadow Bridge, which Reece said was the coolest she'd ever seen. We'd camouflaged the bridge with paint and vines and rocks so that it looked like a natural bridge. The road wasn't the best, and we had to stop a few places to reroute. But slow and sure we made it all the way to Devil's Cranium. Near the Bone Tree, I built a fire. (I checked with Officer Taylor about making the fire. No need to press my luck.) We had a cooler full of food and drinks. It would be our last powwow as a five-member clan. The night was calm, the sky so clear you could see the Milky Way. I tried to be cheerful, but it was hard with Reece and Mei working just to keep from bawling.

Mei had made albums for each of us with pictures of the past year: us working on *The Adventures of Tom Sawyer,* the Chicago trip to the Stallards' office and museum, us goofing off in Council Cliffs State Park, and a whole lot more—the same images that had flashed through my mind when I was searching for her a few days before. I understood again how much a part of my life Mei had been. She was the hands of our clan, the artist. She was also the peace, bringing quiet calm to all of us.

We took a long while looking over the pictures and having laughs.

Rob was still grinning when we finished eating; he had something up his sleeve. Skid threw more wood on the fire. When it reached its highest and hottest, Rob stood, spread his arms, and spoke in a thick, formal voice, "Clan of the Fire, this is a sacred moment. We are about to send our sister off into the world. To protect her from the harm of evil, I will now do the sacred dance which our brave Elijah taught us when he conquered the mighty Bloocifer, which our sisters were not so fortunate to witness. So let him of the Tribe of the Sacred Fire receive tribute! Let our noble leader behold . . . the Snake-in-the-Grass Dance! Let the ceremony begin!"

He closed his eyes and started chanting, "Hey-hu-hu-hu. Hey-hu-hu-hu." He bounced twice on each foot, slowly circling the fire. We took up the chant. Skid was grinning at me. Was this the payback he had promised—making fun of me in front of Reece? Whatever. I intended to take it like a man. Once around the fire, Rob nodded to Skid who took off into the darkness.

Round and round Rob went as he told the tale, sounding half Indian, half Gullah preacher: "Brave Warrior hey-hu-hu-HU, he walk the high grass hey-hu-hu-HU. He have eye of eagle hey-hu-hu-HU, and heart of lion hey-hu-hu-HU. He see all, he fear nothing, he so brave ha-ha-HA."

He got more dramatic, bouncing like a bobble head, back and forth as he made up stuff about my bravery, all the while watching for Skid with one eye. "Strongest of the strong, eagle-eye Elijah ha-ha-ha. Swift runner, high leaper, brave ballerina on the plains of Mudjokivi ha-ha-ha."

In a fit of giggles, Reece started beating on the cooler like a tom-tom. Suddenly Skid shot out of the dark, rushed at the campfire and threw a handful of rubber snakes into Rob's path. Rob stopped dead, his hands went up like a jazz dancer. His eyes and mouth popped open in fake shock. The Indian chant caught in his throat. Reece stopped beating. Rob gaped at the snakes and did a little tippy-toe dance. Then like an opera singer, his voice went up ah-AH, ah-AH. He did a couple of ballet spins with his hands in a circle over his head. He ran around like he was barefoot on hot coals, grabbed up the rubber snakes, waved them over his head, and shot off into the night, screaming like a girl.

We laughed our heads off, tears streaming down the girls' faces. But the show wasn't over. I was sitting there getting over my laughing fit when there was a sudden rattling over my head. A terrible shock of cold hit the back of my neck, rushed down my back, and into my jeans. I sucked in air, jumped up with a yell, and spun around.

Skid stood there with a wide, smirky grin on his face and the empty cooler in his hand. "Payback, when you least expected it." I was still gasping from the shock when he came up and slapped me on the back. "Hey, it's only water."

We scooped up the ice to put out the fire, scattered the ashes, loaded up the cart, and drove back slowly through Owl Woods. Halfway through I stopped and cut the lights. We were in total darkness. "You're leaving in the morning?" I asked Mei.

"Yes. Very early."

"So this is good-bye?" It got quiet. "If anyone has anything to say, now's the time."

Skid said, "We love you, girl." His voice was barely a whisper.

Rob said, "You've been great. Magdeline High won't be the same. . . ." His voice faded.

"This will work out," Reece said desperately. "It will. Have faith in God."

Mei sniffled. "I will miss you all . . . you are the best friends I ever had. Thank you for the most wonderful time in my life."

No one said anything for a minute. It was so quiet and dark.

"How do you pray the armor, Reece?" I asked. "Don't you think Mei should have the armor?"

"Yes," she sniffed. After a long minute she prayed, "God, I come . . . we come to you because we are so sad. We don't know why this is happening. But I know from before, when I was hurting so bad in the hospital, that you answer prayers. So, Lord, please fasten the belt of truth on Mei so she'll understand and be able to see the truth. Put the belt of truth on all of us. Thank you for protecting our hearts with your vest of righteousness. Please cover our sins for they are many. Thanks for bringing the shoes to us even though we haven't found them yet, and help us get ready for the road ahead, wherever it leads. And, my Father, even though we've lost the helmet and we haven't found the shield and sword yet, please let Mei understand salvation in her mind, and help her be protected from doubts and fears by faith—faith in you, God. Teach her the power of your Word, the sword. In the name of your Son, Jesus. Amen."

It was quiet again, except for crickets and night sounds.

The whir of wings swept over our heads. Mei gasped. "Just an owl," I said.

"Or a raven," Reece whispered.

Mei sighed. "Thank you for teaching me about God, Reece. I know he is real. I have felt him in my heart when he took away your pain. He answered my prayer in the park when Elijah came, when I—" A cry caught in her throat. "I hope you find the shoes of peace."

I said to Mei, "I hope you find peace too. We'll pray for each other—to God." I emphasized God. I wanted to make that clear.

It was Rob's idea for Francine Groves/Dowland and Bruce Theobald to make peace. After what happened to his family, Rob was strong on people working things out.

Rob had Aunt Grace invite Francine to stay at the Wingate Bed and Breakfast and Tea Room. As the first customer, she received a free introductory offer. Not all the bedrooms were done, but they had to start turning a profit. Aunt Grace hoped that Francine would take a stack of brochures back to Kentucky.

Francine Groves got settled in by 2:00, and at 4:00 Bruce Theobald stepped into the foyer in plaid shirt and jeans, looking like a bull in a china shop and figuring he was coming to give quotes on a bulldozing job or digging a new sewer line or something.

"Don't anybody flash a red hankie and yell *Toro!*" I whispered from the kitchen. Rob got the joke and snorted. Reece stayed in the kitchen while Rob took Skid and me up the stairs and made us hide in his room so we wouldn't ruin the "ambience." He was jittery, but straightening himself like a butler, he knocked on Francine's door and said, "Someone is downstairs to see you, ma'am. And we have tea for you in the parlor."

She came out. "Why, how sweet." Rob was so into the drama, and Francine ate it up.

When she got to the bottom of the steps, she saw Theobald standing there impatiently looking at pictures on the wall. Rob said, "I think you two have something to talk about."

It took a minute to register with them both. Francine took a step forward, as if her eyes were failing. "Bruce?"

Theobald answered with a curse of disbelief. Aunt Grace showed up on cue. (All of a sudden it sank in with me where Rob got his acting talent. She played her part to the hilt.) She pulled out chairs at a table and said, "Please have a seat. Tea is on the house."

Bruce looked like he wanted to make a break for it, but Rob stood in the doorway and said, "Mr. Theobald, Ms. Groves, it's time to make peace with the past."

The talk started slow and awkward, and we didn't want to eavesdrop. Well, we did want to, but Aunt Grace wouldn't let us.

We could overhear a little as Francine told Bruce how she had never been opposed to his seeing her daughter until they got too involved. About how she couldn't bear to stay in Magdeline. They mumbled about Stan's iron fist and Kate and the baby. By the time seconds on scones came around, Bruce was blowing his nose into the linen napkin, and Francine was patting his arm.

Rob put his hand up and gave me a silent high five.

Skid whispered, "You should forget the storm chasing and go into family therapy." He shrugged. "Or both. Interesting double major—meteorology and psychotherapy—but if anyone could pull it off, it'd be you, Wingate."

When it was all over, we came out for what felt like a curtain call. We wheeled Reece out from the kitchen. Francine thanked us.

Bruce blustered, "This was a nice thing you did. I appreciate the trouble you went to. The town ain't been easy on you."

Rob blushed and said it was nothing.

"You ever need a favor, I'll give you a deal," said Bruce.

Aunt Grace shook her head, but I stepped in. "Favor? Like what?"

He shrugged. "I dunno. Basement dug."

"You mean like a heavy machinery favor? Because if that's what you mean—well, you know that hunk of land behind the camp? We've been working on a road back there, but it still has some rough spots."

"I couldn't get to it until September," Bruce said.

"That'd be okay," I said. "You could do in a few hours what would take us weeks. That'd be awesome!"

Before we left, I had a few loose ends to tie up with Francine. "Um, ma'am, what did you mean about that reject grave being yours?"

"I was dead to Stan, that's all I meant. He wrote me off. He got so caught up in the mystery of that armor and running the church his way, nothing else mattered."

I gave it one more shot. "So you don't know where any of it might be? The shield? The sword?"

"Sword? There never was a sword."

"There has to be a sword," Reece said. She turned to me and whispered, "The sword is the Word of God!"

Francine Groves made a thin-lipped smile. "Honey, it's a piece of junk with Bible words engraved on it. Don't make the same mistake Stan did."

Francine went back up to her room, and we four went out to The Castle's spiffy new porch.

I said, "There has to be a sword if it's the armor of God. Right?"

"It is!" Reece agreed. "Otherwise we wouldn't have been led to the pieces like we were."

"I wouldn't have learned about the truth the way I did," I said.

"My parents got together because I wore it," said Rob.

"Hold on," Skid objected. "Your parents got back together because you showed them the light of day."

I said, "Maybe Francine just forgot. It's been a long time."

Skid said, "I know where we can find out. Florence's."

We looked at him.

"Old church members who saw the armor standing in the church. They'd remember if it had a sword. Excellent idea," he congratulated himself.

I said, "You're just addicted to grits, man. That's the real reason you keep going back."

"What if . . . ," Rob began, "what if it got left in that shop in Ireland?"

Chapter 21

REECE was a basket case after Mei left. I had to get her out of the house and into nature. "Hey, we never checked the rim trail of the first site. I think the shoes have to be at Council Cave."

"No," she said, "I can't . . ."

"You can stay in the gorge in your wheelchair. We'll circle the top. Should only take an hour or so."

"I'll be more trouble than I'm worth."

"I know, but I'm starting to like trouble. Trouble's okay with me. The shoes have to be in the park. The raven led us there."

As we unloaded the wheelchair at Council Cave, Reece said, "Well, here we are back where we started—in the place of the bad news of war. Without Mei."

We went slowly on the path, reminiscing about Mei— how she'd been so excited about school and getting her driver's license. A few trees in the gorge were tinged with red already. The chill in the air and the smell of fall . . . brought a kind of energy surging up in me. I couldn't give up the search, no matter what Francine Groves said. I just couldn't.

We settled Reece in a sunny spot near the falls, circled the rim, and came back down—empty-handed.

Determined, I said, "You know, we could do one more sweep of the gorge. We haven't gone over every single—"

"Give it up, Creek," Skid said.

"I must have missed a sign," I said, looking up at the disk of blue sky encircled by the sandstone ledge.

Reece said, "Maybe we have to think about what we've learned before we find the shoes."

The falls were a trickle, the sandy pool just a puddle. Reece took a deep breath. "It is so peaceful here. And I'm at peace about Mei. God will work it out."

"We did solve the illegal fires mystery, and those lazy counselors are packing their bags. Rob, you have to lie low. No showing your face at Camp Mudj until the coast is clear."

Rob laughed. "I almost blew our cover when you came running across the camp with Bloocifer's babies. If the counselors hadn't been sleeping in, they'd have seen me for sure." He paused. "Maybe we should tell them—make 'em feel dumb."

I shook my head. "Better that they think a wounded bear and some trigger-happy townspeople are roaming the countryside."

We chuckled.

"I don't feel real peaceful about Bloocifer," I admitted. "I have her babies, but she's still on the loose."

"But you're going to make some money off those snakes."

"Yeah . . ."

The wet, sandy water carried a whiff of Farr Island beach. I mentioned it to the guys, and they agreed.

"Francine made peace with Theobald," Reece said. "Rob, that was so cool of you."

Skid said, "Did a good thing, Wingate. A good thing."

"Where do we go from here?" I hesitated to ask since I'm the leader.

Reece said, "I don't know, but I'm at peace about what will happen to me. It's part of my adventure. When I think of those two boys, the hermits, and what they went through, my troubles seem small. Somehow that gives me peace."

Skid said, "Maybe Mei found God here in her answered prayer."

I said, "Well, I guess let's go. Mom'll be here soon."

Mom pulled off the road and came over with a notebook in her arm. "How'd it go?" she asked, looking at Reece with concern.

"Fine," Reece said. "I'm so glad to be outside in the world."

Mom said, "Elijah, your dad needs me to get a few leaf samples from the gorge for his nature talk this afternoon. It'll just take a minute. You can be helping Reece into the car." She took off and then turned. "Oh, there's a package in the car. It came for you today. It was too big for the mailbox, so I had to stop by the post office. And a letter too, marked 'Urgent' from the Stallards. A real rush on mail today. I'll be right back."

It was the size of a big shoe box—the kind you get boots in—fairly heavy and wrapped in grocery bag paper. It was addressed to me. The return address was Francine Groves, Cordova, Kentucky.

"Open it!" Reece said.

I plopped down on the ground in front of Reece and tore into the paper. Rob kneeled down beside me. Skid hovered over Reece's shoulder.

My hands trembled. "It *is* a shoe box!" I tore off the lid. There, underneath a handwritten note, was a pair of old, heavy sandals. Slowly I lifted them out. They had thick soles and rugged leather straps trimmed with metal. "The shoes of peace!"

"They could be Roman," Rob said in awe.

"The shoes of peace!" Reece reached out. I put one in her hands. "The word," she said eagerly. "Where's the word?"

Rob helped me examine the shoe. "Hey, look, the laces are thin strips of braided leather."

Skid said, "'A cord of three strands is not quickly broken.' It's Mei's favorite Scripture."

Reece touched the laces sadly. "I may never see her again."

"Sure you will," I said. "Have faith."

She nodded and bit her lip.

Skid squatted beside her. "Hey now, girl. Hard times come. The next piece is the shield of faith, so we gotta have faith." He pointed up. "Take it to Command Central."

She nodded. "I'll be okay."

A strip of metal going calf-high up the back of the shoe was carved with beautiful whirls and circles. "Maybe the word is encoded in the design!"

None of us could find anything that looked like letters.

"Here it is. On the sole!" Reece said. The leather trim along the sole was so scratched, I'd missed it. "English letters on the outside edge. It says *langun . . . dow . . . langundow.* If there's more I can't read it."

I rubbed dust off the outer edge. "There is more. It says *langun . . . dowagan. Langundowagan.* Sounds Indian!"

"You think everything is Indian," Rob teased. "Here's what the note says:

Dear young people, I can't remember all your names, I am sorry. Here are the shoes. Since you were so kind and helpful to me, I couldn't keep this secret. When Stan and I had our last fight, I saw pieces of the armor at the house. What he was doing with them I'll never know. We got into another disagreement over it, as we had so many times before.

When he got upset and went into the kitchen to get his medication, I took the shoes. I wanted to make him suffer for all the pain he'd caused me. I wish I hadn't. I wonder now if it was the loss of these shoes that sent him into his final rage. I don't know what Stan did with the rest. On my word I don't.

My husband believed a story that the armor held the secret to a rare, priceless treasure. He became obsessed with the idea of becoming wealthy so he could get revenge on those who betrayed him, but after researching every possible lead, he came up with nothing.

Many times over the last few days, I thought of throwing these sandals out. But I couldn't bring myself to do it. I haven't slept well keeping secrets all these years. These sandals are my last secret. Thank you for helping me set things right with Bruce. I feel so much better now. The shoes are yours, but don't make the same mistake my husband did.

You seem like such nice kids, and you have your whole lives ahead of you. Don't waste them. I've done what I thought best. Now I can rest in peace. Best of Luck and God Bless, Francine Groves.

Rob looked around at us mysteriously. "She found peace too."

Skid tore open the letter from the Stallards. "Okay, here's that list the Stallards sent: *peace* in every language. Pretty impressive: *a paz* (Portuguese), *achukma* (Choctaw), *amani* (Swahili) . . ."

"Look at the *L*s," Reece said.

"Here it is! *Langundowagan.* It's the Lenape word for peace."

Rob's head shot up. "Lenape? The language of the Delaware Indians!"

I stood up and paced. "How in the world did an Indian word get on shoes that came from the Middle East and were found in Ireland before Stan bought them a few decades ago—all the way back here, where the Delawares lived!!?"

"How in the world, exactly!" Skid said.

"Guys," Reece said, her voice low and suspenseful, "guys, do you know what just happened? We found the shoes of the readiness of the good news of peace in a war council site."

"Actually," I said in disbelief, "the shoes found us! They found us in the first place we thought they'd be. And this time it wasn't Stan Dowland who decided where they should be."

Rob gasped. He turned to me. "Your mom didn't know we were looking here for—"

"No."

Reece said, "This is the first piece Dowland didn't bury; it wasn't in *his* place of war. But it *was* a place of war between nations. A bigger war."

"Nation against nation, tribe against tribe."

"And a place where people came to find peace." Reece's face was strong and smiling now. "You know what this means? We're no longer following Dowland's signs."

She looked up at the clouds and smiled. "God's been guiding us all along, just using Dowland. He alone is guiding us now."

We rode back into town in silence, each one keeping to his thoughts.

Mom dropped Reece off. As soon as I got home, I called her, knowing she'd pick up the phone. "Big question," I said.

"Okay . . ."

"If God knows where all the pieces are, why doesn't he just tell us outright? We've been going at this almost a year now."

She thought a minute. "I don't know. Maybe he's teaching us to have faith."

"Faith?"

"Yeah. He wants us to trust him every step of the way. And maybe he's training us too."

"Training for what?" There was a long pause. "You still there, Reece?"

"Hold on, I'm trying to put the pieces together."

"What pieces?"

"You know, the mystery of Old Pilgrim Church, Dowland's story, the maps and research, all of us turning out best friends—"

I filled in more, "The jungle training—which we've already used a couple of times—the natural disasters which led us to the next piece—"

"Divorces and dead ends and pain—"

"Near suicides and danger." And I added, "Wild animals."

"I think I know what you're going to say, Elijah."

"War?" I said, with chills going up my spine.

"That's just what I was thinking. He's training us for war."

THE HAUNTED SOUL

I was reaching my hand into the fire, trying to snatch something out of it. My mom screamed at me, but I kept saying, "I'm okay, I'm okay!" I wasn't being burned, but they didn't believe me. "I'm okay!" I insisted.

"Elijah?" Mom's worried voice called to me as if from far away. She shook me awake. "You were having a nightmare. Elijah, hon, it's all right. You're in your room."

I sat up—my head wobbling, my eyelids drooping. "Yeah . . . I dreamed I was reaching into a fire, and you were yelling at me."

"Dad needs you at the nature center as soon as you can get there, but it's not an emergency," she tousled my hair. "It's a good thing."

"'Kay." I forced my eyes open and surveyed the backyard and beyond. Through my open window, I saw the pool, as quiet and blue as the sky above. Beyond lay a plot of bare land. The Camp Mudjokivi trustees had bought up the spot that once was Old Pilgrim Church. Dad wanted to make it into a sand volleyball court for next summer—his idea being to attract college kids for twilight shindigs around the pool while campers trekked through Owl Woods on night hikes. I rubbed sleep from my eyes. "It's almost 9:00 already?"

Mom looked at her watch. "Exactly ten minutes till. I'll never know how you tell time like that. You can't even see the sun from your window."

I shrugged and blinked. "I dunno . . . the color of the sky, the smell of the air after the dew burns off . . ." I threw back the covers and stood, swaying like a drunk. "I'm okay."

Mom laughed. "You said that already. Dorian just called and asked me to drop by right away. He sounded mysterious on the phone." She walked out of the room, twisting her hair up and clipping it. "It's probably nothing. He loved teasing me as a kid. My brother, the bane of my existence!"

School was set to start in a week, and I dreaded it more than usual. The five of us had spent half the summer roaming Council Cliffs State Park. Roaming: it's what I like best in the world. Then Reece got hurt. The doctors had to cut a bone out of her leg, sand it off, and put it back in. No one could believe how soon she was up and around, though still on crutches all the time. Mei had been sent back to Japan by her parents who thought we were some weird religious cult for kids. According to Reece, Mei's parents had found some ideas for clan names that Mei had written in her journal, names like Secret Society of Telanoo, Clan of Fire, Warriors of Gi, Fighters for God. To an outsider this might seem weird, but we were just regular kids looking for an old suit of armor with the power and history of spiritual warfare tied up in it. Mei's parents didn't understand. They tried to get her to break off from our group. When she wouldn't budge, they shipped her back to Japan.

Reece missed Mei a bunch, and our clan was down to four again: Reece, Skid, Rob, and me. I didn't get why God couldn't fix everything. Several times I'd even asked, *Why are you doing this to Reece—taking her friends away, keeping her on crutches? She trusts you. You're number one with her. Doesn't that count for something?* I even said once, *Hey, if that's what it means to be on your A-Team, no thanks.*

Dad met me in the reptile room of the nature center, wearing his usual khakis and Camp Mudj T-shirt. "We have buyers, Elijah."

I perked up. "For the baby snakes?"

"Yes."

"Cool!" We high fived.

"The money's yours, son."

"Really?! How much?" I peeked in on the writhing mass of speckled blue racer babies which were under maximum security alert with a padlocked cage and a sign on the reptile room door: "Authorized Personnel Only"—which meant Dad, Bo, and me.

Dad admired our stash of rare snakes. "We're still dickering on the price," he answered.

"Dicker high, okay?"

"You earned it, Elijah." He broke into a chuckle. "You know what *I'd* pay cold cash for: seeing you tear up the hill again—your fists full of baby blues—and Rob bounding sideways into the lake like a human pogo stick." He paused to picture it and laughed out loud. "No sooner had he hit water than he was out of it again."

"When Rob goes spastic, he goes whole hog." I thanked Dad again and headed back to the house. My dad's the greatest—ever. I want to make that clear before I tell this next part. I don't mean anything bad by this, but after that one night earlier in the summer when he couldn't answer my questions about God and the other world out there, something clicked in my head. Not disappointment but a shift in my thinking. Dad didn't have all the answers, especially answers to questions that I'd come to think were pretty important. I needed to know.

"Can I borrow that Quella sometime?" I asked Skid when we met by accident at the grocery store. We were loading up on school supplies. Being a man of action more than a man of words, I'd hardly used a pencil and paper all summer, so my errand was more for the twins. They needed glue and colored pencils, and they'd graduated from those round scissors to the pointy, dangerous ones. I hoped Mom was ready to part with her good drapes, the shower curtain, pages from her favorite ladies' magazines, and anything else a blade could go through.

"The Quella?" Skid asked. "Sure. Why?"

"Well," I stammered, getting shy all of a sudden, "You guys keep bugging me about church. I want to know what I'm getting into beforehand."

He pulled it out of his jacket pocket and handed it over to me without a hitch. "Look up *saved*, Creek. That's what you're shooting for."

"Okay. Thanks."

Later that week—almost a year since we'd first gone into Old Pilgrim Church—I went up on Devil's Cranium and built a little fire, just enough to read by. This wasn't a vision quest; I was learning that God's showing up didn't depend on you sweating and showering and starving yourself. You could knock yourself out, and he might leave you sitting there in the dead quiet to think it out all alone. It was his call. Reece thought he'd be showing up in the Word to tell us what to do next, which was good enough for me.

It was funny, reading about saved in the Bible. There were a bunch of short paragraphs in different parts to hunt down and ponder a long time. It wasn't like a schoolbook. Learning about saved was kind of like my first prayer walk, only I wasn't walking a snake-infested meadow at dawn.

In Matthew's book it said, "He will save his people from their sins."

Sins? Well, God, I used to lie, but I've steered away from it after finding the belt of truth. As for other sins, I haven't killed anyone except Salem. I haven't stolen anything except for that leather key ring from Mitt's Bros. Department Store when Aunt Grace worked there. Once was all, and I lost the key ring the next day at school. I was seven and dumb at the time. Sorry 'bout that.

"Whoever wants to save his life will lose it, but whoever loses his life for me will find it."

Huh? What's that mean? I'll have to ask Reece or Skid.

James's book said, "What good is it, my brothers, if a man claims to have faith but has no deeds? Can such faith save him?"

"For it is by grace you have been saved, through faith," was in Ephesians.

Then in the book of Romans, it said, "If you confess with your mouth, 'Jesus is Lord,' and believe in your heart that God raised him from the dead, you will be saved." I sat there in the mellow twilight of late summer and pondered the words.

From high on Devil's Cranium, I looked across Telanoo, which I had fully claimed as my own. No one else wanted it, no one used it, and I'd covered pretty much all of it looking for the armor. If I got creeped out—like the time I heard a coyote at sundown on the west perimeter, or the time of the cloudburst when visibility went to nothing and I lost my way—I'd call to El-Telan-Yah: a name I made meaning "the God of Telanoo is Yahweh."

Ancient Truth

※※※

(Page 6) "Though I walk through the valley of the shadow of death, I will fear no evil, for you are with me."

Psalm 23:4

(Page 19) "And with your feet fitted with the readiness that comes from the gospel of peace."

Ephesians 6:15

(Page 175) "Though one may be overpowered, two can defend themselves. A cord of three strands is not quickly broken."

Ecclesiastes 4:12

Creek Code

〰〰〰〰〰〰〰〰〰〰〰〰〰〰〰〰〰〰〰〰〰〰〰〰〰〰〰〰〰〰〰〰〰〰〰

Japanese

Daijoubu—(die-jo-boo) It's all right

Gi—(ghee) A kanji character meaning righteousness

Kimoi—(kee-moh-ee) Gross

Moshi moshi—(moh-shee moh-shee) Hello (used only when speaking on telephone)

Muzukashii—(moo-zoo-kah-shee-ee) Difficult

Shinkansen—(sheen-kahn-sen) The Bullet Train

Sugoi—(soo-goy) Wow

Taihen—(tie-hen) Terrible; very, etc.

Delaware

Langundowagan—(lahn-goon-do-wah-gahn) Peace

Hebrew

Omen—(awlef mame noon)—Truth, faithfulness

Y'shua Meshiach—(y'-shoo-ah me-shee-akh) Jesus Messiah

Council Cliffs State Park

※※※

COUNCIL Cliffs State Park really exists! The park's real name is Hocking Hills. The main entrance of the park is located on Route 664 in south-central Ohio—kind of off the beaten track.

I changed the names of the sites so I could fiddle with the topography if I wanted to, but in general you'll find that Hermits' Cave is really Old Man's Cave. A hermit named Richard Rowe is said to have lived there for many years. Cathedral Cave is really Rock House, the northernmost site in Hocking Hills. And Council Cave is Ash Cave. There is no Lover's Leap that I know of. (The only leap lovers of God should take is the leap of faith.)

If your family gets a chance to travel through Ohio, take a day to see a few of the beautiful gorges of Hocking Hills. The photo on the front cover was taken there. You can find more information about the park online.

Three cities of peace were established in Ohio in the 1700s, but a deceitful plot by a white army wiped them out. As for the Moravian Delawares, the story of the massacre and the narrow escape of two boys is true, though details in different accounts vary. About the fate of the two boys: I could find no account of what happened to them. I imagine it was hard for them to trust anyone after what they suffered. I hope they found peace.

—Lena Wood